Red-Tailed Rescue

Red-Tailed Rescue

John Irby

For Terri,
A dearest friend and someone who spread her wings wide and flew wide so that her students could fly ever higher.
Love,
John E. Irby
2014

WiDō Publishing
Salt Lake City • Houston

WiDō Publishing
Salt Lake City, Utah
www.widopublishing.com

Copyright © 2014 by John Irby

All rights reserved. No part of this book may be reproduced or transmitted in any form or by any means, electronic or mechanical, including photocopying, recording, or by any information storage and retrieval system, without the written consent of the publisher.

Cover Design by Steven Novak
Book Design by Marny K. Parkin

ISBN: 978-1-937178-46-8
Library of Congress Control Number: 2013958278
Printed in the United States of America

OR MY MOTHER, VIOLA GRACE, WHO SHOVED ME toward the books.

Also, for thirty Septembers of students—most willing, some not—at Kenmore Junior High.

But especially for my children, Johnny, Tobi Anne, and Amber, who still love a good story.

E NEED ANOTHER AND A WISER AND PERHAPS a more mystical concept of animals.

We patronize them for their incompleteness, For their tragic fate of having taken form so far below ourselves, and therein we err, and greatly err.

They are not brethren, they are not underlings, they are other nations, caught in the net of life and time, fellow prisoners of the splendor and travail of the earth.

The Outermost House
Henry Beston

Chapter One

The Accident

ORVILLE, A MAGNIFICENT RED-TAILED HAWK, floated effortlessly, precisely six hundred and fifty feet above five thousand acres of brownish green, South Dakota ranchland, just south of the Moreau River in Ziebach County.

Above him curled the crust of the universe, endless indigo blue. Orville's flight plan was a routine, simple circle, perhaps a half-mile in diameter, getting slightly smaller at each go round. Below him was the Flannery home, a two-story white affair, ringed by an emerald green lawn, various leafy shade trees, and tidy flower gardens. A black Ford pick-up truck and a dusty white, Toyota Corolla four-door sedan were parked next to the house.

From Orville's vantage high overhead, he was vaguely aware of David and Elizabeth Flannery's home and road equipment. He was, however, acutely mindful of a brown, whitetail rabbit contentedly munching on some succulent lettuce plants growing near the back porch. The bunny had been in Orville's sights for ten minutes or longer and had no inkling of the hawk's presence—or his intent.

Nearby, off to one side, about twenty yards apart, in full sun, stood two wooden posts with braced crosspieces. Between the posts were strung three strands of clothesline wire, which today, sagged under the weight of Beth Flannery's morning wash. The drying clothes barely fluttered in the gentle breeze, but the unrelenting late summer sun's rays created a dazzling reflection off the white articles.

Orville's orbits continued to grow tighter to the target with each pass, but he maintained his altitude at the specific surveillance height. The mild, mid-day wind held no importance to the matter. The various attack options and descent calculations already considered, he patiently waited for the optimum moment.

Kate Flannery, thirteen come September, opened the back door, leaped from the top step of the wooden porch to the soft grass four feet below, landed, and immediately performed a cartwheel. The young rabbit, startled by the sudden boisterous activity, froze and hugged the ground. Meanwhile, Kate, willow thin, dressed in a white tank top and yellow shorts, cartwheeled her bare-footed self like a runaway Ferris wheel around the house to the more shaded west side. Her long, reddish-blonde braid slapped her lower back with each graceful circle.

In the shade beneath the eighty-year-old apple tree her great-grandfather had planted to honor his new bride on their wedding day lay a rather tattered, brown Army blanket—a prized relic from her grandfather's Army days, a black boom-box-type portable radio, and a stack of five library books carted home the previous day from Dupree, the county seat, some twenty-five dusty miles due south.

A faint primer coat of drying milk painted the gentle ridge above Kate's upper lip. A tiny clump of raspberry jam and peanut butter clung stubbornly to one corner of her mouth. Lunch to Kate was just a momentary interruption from her favorite pastime on planet Earth—reading.

She devoured book after book all summer vacation long, grabbing them from the library shelves almost at random. A quick glance would tell her two things—this was fresh material and the subject matter did not include her reading allergies of murder or war.

Sometimes the town librarian, Miriam Koppel, kept aside a new book or two, saved special, just for Kate. When Kate hurried to the library's checkout counter lugging a pile of books, Ms. Koppel would often turn around and produce one or two others from the shelf behind her workspace. She'd say, her voice and smile betraying her fondness, "Kate, I wonder if you'd mind test-driving these new arrivals for me? They just came in a few days ago, and I haven't had time to read them yet."

The truth was Miriam Koppel had three sprouting children and a husband at home to care for, blue ribbon rhubarb pies to bake, and quilts to sew for display at the upcoming county fair, a rambling house to keep, and a garden the size of a tennis court to weed. It was a distinct irony the town librarian, devoted to the reading needs of the community, had precious little spare time of her own to read books intended for middle-grade children and young adults. To help fill the gap, Kate had become one of the library's test drivers for new books.

Kate would beam widely, revealing a pair of curved parentheses-like dimples at the corners of her lips. "Cool. Be glad to, Ms. Koppel," she'd say. "Thanks for thinking of me."

By the end of the third chapter, if the plot were slow or the characters dull, she'd gently close the book, almost as if to not offend the author, move it to the bottom of the stack, saved for later, and eagerly open a fresh volume.

Mostly though, Kate enjoyed every page of every book; the trail of words hiking adventurously across the page, strung together to form interesting ideas, wafted her magically, like a hawk's wings, out from under a lovely shade tree and away from the—don't blink or you'll miss it—town of Dupree, South Dakota.

As soon as her chores were complete, she had begun reading a novelette called *The Cat and the Coffee Drinkers* recommended by Kate's sixth grade teacher, Ms. Flatt. Her first name was Doris, but no student dared address her in such a casual manner. On the school playground, out of earshot, some of the bolder boys referred to their teacher as Notso—a naughty reference to Ms. Flatt's mountainous boobs. She had blocked the door of the classroom on the last day of school before summer break, arms extended up and wide like tilted goalposts, inviting a soft farewell *All is forgiven* hug, and a murmured, "I'm going to miss you so much." But, before a clean escape could be made, she handed a seventh grade Suggested Summer Reading List to each student as they filed past. On her way to the parking lot, with a dark cloud upon her face, Ms. Flatt scooped up a dozen or more of her summer reading lists littering the school grounds.

The Cat and the Coffee Drinkers was one of twenty titles listed on Ms. Flatt's sheet. At the library, Ms. Koppel had to special order the book for Kate, clear from Rapid City. By then Kate had already dispatched the other nineteen on the list, plus another five or so of her own choosing, not to mention several of Ms. Koppel's test-drive books.

Kate's curious blues, shaded by airy lashes the color of sun-baked corn silk, sparkled as she lovingly turned the pages of *The Cat and the Coffee Drinkers.* A persistent grin tugged at her lips as she read how Miss Effie, the kindergarten coffee drinkers' teacher, in her unique, dictatorial way, had taught the boys to be polite and capable gentlemen, and the girls to be proper and useful young ladies. But, Kate's eyes had filled with tears when Miss Effie dismissed the students early one day because the one lesson she had to teach them was how to kill a cat. A cat the teacher pretended to dislike, but in fact loved with all her heart.

Kate slowly closed the book on her chest, rubbed her eyes with the side of her forefinger, and gazing up through leafy branches of the old apple tree, planted out of love, contemplated through wet eye lashes the sorrow someone feels who must end a beloved pet's life in order to prevent more suffering.

Then her thoughts shifted to a time, two years before, when Gramma Flannery had sat beside Grampa's bed for four days and nights at Hans P. Peterson Memorial Hospital down in Philip. Right after breakfast each morning, Kate and her mom and dad had driven down to Phillip to check on Gramma and Grampa. When Kate would follow her parents into the room, Gramma would be reading aloud to Grampa. He remained unresponsive, eyes closed, hands folded peacefully over his tummy, but Gramma's soft voice never faltered. On the last morning, when Kate and her parents arrived, a large red Do Not Enter sign was taped to the closed door.

After a moment of whispered discussion, the nurse on duty gave them permission to open the door. For the first time, the room was almost perfectly silent save for the distant hum of the hospital air-conditioner. Gramma had climbed onto the bed and tenderly cradled her husband's head in her arms. A worn copy of Shakespeare's sonnets lay mute on the chair. Kate's parents leaned awkwardly over the bed and hugged Gramma as best they could. Kate stood rooted at the foot of the bed, white-faced and hollow-eyed. *Surely*, she thought, *this was how Miss Effie felt the day she taught her students how to kill a cat.*

Through eyes misty with memory, Kate saw a dark meteor with a flash of molten red, heard a loud thump, and a shrill cry of pain. She did not yet realize it, but

Orville, plummeting at one hundred forty miles per hour through the brilliant South Dakota sky, blinded by Beth Flannery's gloriously clean laundry, had caught a wing tip on one of the wires, cartwheeled, and plastered himself into the side of the house. He landed a few feet away from Dave Flannery's discarded work boot and sock—a sock that was the white-tailed rabbit Orville had attacked.

Chapter Two
High Hopes

The day dawned achingly clear. The sun, a brilliant ball of crimson smoldered low in the east; the sky, still inky, muted the dazzling light; the wind not yet formed, stirred not at all.

Most of South Dakota still slept, but the young hawks, up early, perched nervously below their teacher on the lower branches of a long dead cottonwood near a dry creek bed perhaps a mile from their schoolhouse.

Their teacher, RT Boyd Higgins, had slept at the test site, on his back, talons pointing upward as if to pluck the shimmering peach-like moon from the sky, his wings spread across the V formed by joined branches high above the ground. He had slept soundly, convinced this graduating class, no doubt the best group of students in his long teaching career, would meet all the flight standards required by the state to earn their temporary Conditional Attack diplomas. He was hopeful a few, perhaps two or three out of the thirty, would surpass the rigorous state requirements and be selected as Commended Flyers of the South Dakota Hawk Squadron.

He had the highest of hopes for Lindy, a flawless navigator and the best young female flyer he'd ever seen; for Orville, a fearless flyer and the brainiest by far; and marginally for Amelia, a vibrant beauty with unmatched endurance and an instinct for flying rarely seen among young hawks these days. Dare he dream of such honors? In his twelve years of teaching, not one of his previous students had earned exceptional Commended Flyer status.

Baby hawks, "fledglings" they're called, can indeed fly within six weeks of their hatching, but the extraordinary skills required to hunt—to float on a mere zephyr, to spot the prey, stalk, calculate, accelerate, and dive at breakneck speed, brake, stun, and snatch an unwary victim—these skills required extensive training, strength, courage, and patience.

Fifteen years earlier, Boyd Higgins had flown with the storied Silver Feathers, an elite hawk security squadron, for two years before snapping his left wing executing an Assassin's Spiral against a marauding eagle over by Lacreek Lake, near the town of Tuthill, just north of the Nebraska border. Even with the best possible medical care and months of tedious rehabilitation, his wing never regained full strength. With great regret, he had resigned his posting rather than bring almost certain disgrace to his flying mates.

What to do? His small medical pension would barely pay the rent. Newly married, how could he possibly support his wife? No employer in his right mind would consider hiring him—a disabled flyer.

As luck would have it, the day Higgins reluctantly signed his discharge papers, just as he was about to wing off, Captain Percy Douthwaite, his squad leader, suggested he go into teaching.

"Have a go at it, lad," Captain Douthwaite said. "Boyd, you've got everything it takes to be a great teacher." His gold eyes had glittered in the morning sun.

"Teach them how to really fly, Higgins. Send us a fledgling just like you were the day you winged in from Kadoka. No one could dive like you, Higgins!"

Boyd Higgins had never known Percy to lavish unmerited praise on any hawk before, so he took his kind words and sound advice to heart. Less than an hour later, he and his new bride flew home from the academy for the first time in nearly six months. His mother fattened them with home-cooked meals and his father, a retired Sky Patrol officer, helped Boyd fill out the application forms. Before the month was out, RT Boyd Higgins had been accepted at the famous Hawk Institute of Aeronautics up in the state capitol, Pierre. To this day he suspected Captain Douthwaite had an influential wing in on his quick appointment.

Two years later with the ink not yet dry on his master's degree, he began his teaching internship at Snake Butte Flight School, near Potato Creek down south in Jackson County. After his year of internship, he found a permanent teaching slot up north at a small public school, Prairie Winds School of Flight. The school was less than ten miles from the tiny community of Iron Lightning, nestled against the Moreau River, a prime grazing and hunting area.

When Higgins arrived, the Prairie Winds' curriculum in mathematics and terrain geography was not, to put it delicately, adequate. These were hard-working, no-nonsense, blue-collar hawks. They were in the air at dawn seven days a week, and scoured the territory until dwindling dusk made it too dangerous to fly. But, and this was vital, they did not grasp the critical correlation between mathematics and hunting success, nor did they value the significance of terrain expertise. Iron Lightning hawks, like all red-tails, have courage, vision, instinct, and wing strength in abundance. Also, their tenacious willingness to tackle whatever it took to get the job done properly was legendary throughout the state.

As Higgins evaluated the situation, the job, it seemed to him, was to take his students' already superior natural flying heritage, emphasize math and geography, coupled with their outstanding work ethic, and produce some of the finest young flyers South Dakota had ever seen. Idealistic? Perhaps, but the newly minted teacher Boyd Higgins, himself no longer able to fly with reckless abandon, was determined to help nourish young flyers who could.

Twelve years later, here he was, flat on his back enjoying a fiery sunrise in an old cottonwood tree with a giddy flock of superbly talented fledglings gathered beneath him. Somewhere below, Lindy, Orville, Amelia, and the others waited for their opportunity to bring indescribable honor to their school, their community, themselves, and, of course, in a roundabout way, to their teacher. What Higgins would have given to be able to fly like these three once more.

Chapter Three
Oh Well

HAWKS AND HUMANS, FAR BACK IN TIME, HAD intertwined hearts. Before any mechanical contraptions were built to make survival easier, humans spent the greater part of every day, from the first glimmer of light until dusk, trying to find shelter for the night. While they searched, they foraged with their bare hands for food of any kind. They caught and ate what living creatures they could—from the sea, rivers, lakes, the land, and from the sky. They also combed bushes, trees, flowers, and every inch of ground for edible plants, seeds, and berries.

Some of what they gathered tasted awful. Unless desperately starved, they discarded it. Some were poisonous. Those who ate of it perished, a macabre warning to the others. Historians call these early people "hunters and gatherers." Another appropriate term might be "survivors." Today's hawks, using their talons and beaks, remain, through the unwinding spool of endless time, "hunters, gatherers, and survivors."

As Kate rounded the corner of the house, her dad, Dave Flannery, barefoot, stepped through the back door onto the porch.

"Did you throw something at the house, Kate?" he asked, a puzzled look on his face.

Before she could answer, Orville, coming back to consciousness, let out a shrill cry: "Kiree! Kiree! Kiree!" It was a piercing plea for help, similar to the frantic radio-transmitted, international distress call, "Mayday! Mayday! Mayday!" of WWII pilots about to ditch their aircraft into the sea, mountainside, or forest.

Orville was most certainly assured if there were another hawk within half a mile, a swift rescue team would soon be dispatched.

"It's a hawk, Dad!" Kate shouted.

"Stay back," he ordered, shielding Kate with a protective arm. "I'll get Grampa's shotgun."

"No," she said, "it's injured. Something is wrong with its leg."

At the time of the accident, Orville was rather ordinary in appearance, about two and a half pounds of steely muscle, and perhaps twenty inches long. He was almost three years old and his tail feathers had already turned a brilliant, autumn, maple leaf red.

Orville blinked his eyes rapidly against the bright light and gazed fearlessly up at the pair of humans. He had no way of knowing if his desperate cry for rescue had been picked up off the air currents, but he did know his right leg hurt worse than a festering barbed wire cut on a cold South Dakota morning. Also his left wing felt limp, and he was certain he could not launch himself and gain the airspeed necessary for lift off.

Hawks know not fear, for they live each day, solely because of death. Life and death, to Orville and all hawks, are two luminous threads, one gold and the other silver, exquisitely stitched into the same filigree called existence. Gazing fearlessly up into Kate's face, almost blinded by the afternoon sun, he managed a soft resignation of his fate, "Kuurruft." Oh well. Stuff happens. So it goes.

"Dad, he's trying to tell us something. He won't hurt us. Please don't shoot him." Kate knelt in the soft grass a few feet from Orville.

Just then, Beth Flannery, carrying an empty, plastic laundry basket stepped onto the porch to fetch her dry clothes. "What are you guys doing?" she asked.

"Apparently," Dave replied, pointing at Orville, "this little fella smacked into the house and knocked himself silly. Appears there's something seriously wrong with his leg."

"Why would a hawk fly into the side of our house?" Beth asked. "Crashing doesn't make any sense whatsoever." She faced her husband. "What are you going to do with him?"

Kate eyed her parents. Before her dad could reply she blurted, "Let's drive him to the vet in Dupree. Dr. Walters can fix his leg, and then we can take care of him until he can fly back to his home."

Dave shook his head. "Doc Walters patches up cattle and horses mostly, Kate. I doubt he wants to work on a hawk. Besides, how do we put a wild bird in the truck? I don't think I want to try to pick him up. His beak and talons could do some serious damage if he disagrees with our plan."

Dave removed his green John Deere baseball cap, revealing a secret thin line of bleached white forehead where the South Dakota sun never visited. He scratched his forehead with thick, deeply tanned fingertips. "Maybe we should just leave him be a while. He might be able to fly off on his own."

Beth said, "Are you kidding? The way his leg looks, even if he does fly off he won't live long. Let me try. Kate, go in the house and get my winter work coat and gloves. You know, my old black one in the side closet next to the front door. The gloves should be in the pocket. I'm going to put a towel in this basket for his ride into Dupree."

She reached out and touched her husband's arm. "Will you call the vet on your cell? Just tell him we're coming in with an injured animal. No need to explain it's a wild bird." She flashed a mischievous smile at her husband. "C'mon, hon, this is going to be fun."

Dave Flannery, one of South Dakota's most rugged ranchers, who dealt daily with every discomfort and challenge life on a working ranch dished up, marveled at his petite, yet fearless wife. "Okay, babe," he said. "Watch those big toenails of his though. They're razor sharp."

Orville's senses, dulled somewhat by the shock of his grievous injury, grasped most of what was being said about him. He also realized these humans had somehow understood his simple statement concerning his predicament. He repeated it now: "Kuurruft."

"See," Beth said, "he wants us to help him."

"How in Helena, Montana, do you know that?" Grinning at his wife, Dave's faded blue eyes sparkled with impish disbelief.

"Just the soft tone of his voice. He's not warning us and he's certainly not afraid." Beth skipped down the steps, walked quickly to the clothesline, and unpinned a soft, white bath towel. She folded it in thirds and neatly arranged it across the bottom of the laundry basket.

Kate had returned with her mother's long, heavy coat and the thick winter gloves. Beth put the basket down, slipped her bare arms into the coat, and zipped it up to her chin. Then she pulled on the black leather gloves.

Calmly kneeling in the garden a few feet from Orville, she said, "Hey, little buddy, we're not going to hurt you. Let me pick you up and put you in this basket, okay? Then we'll take you to the doctor and your leg will soon be fixed up as good as new." Her soft voice was reassuring as she inched her hands toward Orville.

Orville lay helplessly on his side and knew his bare defense at this moment was his powerful beak. Normally hawks jolt their prey with a surprise collision, and then capture it with their talons, before winging off. Beth's soothing words kept Orville's talons and beak, at least for now, sheathed.

"Kuurruft," Orville murmured again. He pulled his wings in as tight to his body as possible, blinked his eyes, and patiently awaited his fate. He felt Beth's gloved fingers tenderly cradle his body, lift, and then gently lower him onto the towel. No harm done, though in the transfer, his right leg, bent at an odd angle, dangled grotesquely. A shiver of momentary agony racked his body, but he didn't utter another sound.

"Do you think we should have splinted his leg before you moved him, Mom?" Kate asked. "We were taught to splint broken legs in first-aid class last year."

Beth glanced up at her daughter. "We certainly would have if Gramma had fallen off the porch and broken her hip or something, but I think its best we try not to jostle him anymore than we have to. His leg has got to be on fire. Besides, Gramma probably wouldn't bite us while we splinted her."

Kate giggled. "Don't be too sure. Have you ever seen her sink her fangs into corn on the cob? She gets after it."

Dave said, "Nobody answered at the vet clinic, but Doc could be taking a nap, or maybe he walked home for lunch. I'll put the hawk in the back of the pick-up. We'll give him every chance to escape if he's up to it. He can fly if he wants to."

He took his wife by her shoulders, gently steering her toward the porch. "C'mon, girl, go get your purse and pretty up. We're off to town. Tell Gramma we'll be back in two hours or so." He gave his daughter a playful push. "Hey, Kate, grab your book. Let's go." Dave then sat down on the steps and quickly began pulling a sock onto his stark white, bare foot.

Kate, mind whirling and braid flying, twirled herself back toward her stacked treasury of literature under the sheltering South Dakota apple tree.

Chapter Four
Medical Attention

THE NAMELESS NARROW DIRT ROAD FROM THE Flannery ranch to Dupree lollygags east for a few miles playing tag with the Moreau River, until it reaches the tiny community of Iron Lightning. There it joins the Iron Lightning Road, which turns abruptly south across desolate prairie land toward the town of Red Elm, rooted deep alongside Highway 212. Despite the heavy dust kicked up by the truck's tires, swirling wind, and relentless heat, the air-conditioned ride was still a treat for the three humans. Normally, the Flannerys would routinely drive the Iron Lightning Road into Dupree for groceries, books, or other necessary supplies once a week.

In the back of the pick-up, a helpless but trusting Orville rode perfectly still, each bump of the road causing untold agony. He clamped his beak shut, admirably refusing to voice his pain.

When Dave wheeled up to the vet clinic at the corner of B Street and Elm forty-five minutes later, the small gravel parking lot fronting the low brick building was empty. The temperature had peaked for the day at ninety-six, and the afternoon wind, moodily rambunctious when turned loose, stirred up any trouble it could find.

"Let's go in and talk to Doc first," Dave said, stepping out of the truck. "Maybe he's out on a call or already gone home for the day." He glanced across the seat at Kate. "Or he may not want to mess with a wild hawk."

Kate opened the heavy door and jumped down. She leaned against the side of the truck and peered into the laundry basket. Orville, appearing a bit ruffled, as red-tailed hawks often do, stared curiously back at her.

"You wait here, little buddy," she said, adopting her mother's phrase for Orville. "We have to make sure the doctor is in. Don't you worry now, we'll be right back."

The doctor's office, plainly furnished, but refreshingly cooled by a humming air-conditioner, was empty, save for a small brown sofa, three folding chairs, and a stack of yellow *National Geographic* magazines arranged neatly on a small wooden end table next to the sofa. On the receptionist's counter rested a shiny brass cowbell and propped against it, a small, hand scrawled sign: *Down the street for a coke. Be right back.*

"Doc must have walked uptown. The D.Q. is the closest place cool enough to sit down and drink a coke," Dave said. "You girls wait here. I'm gonna go out and fetch our bird before he gets heat stroke."

But before Dave could take a step the door opened and a slightly stooped, silver-haired gentleman walked in.

"Well, I'll be danged, the Flannery clan has come to town. How are ya, Dave?" He extended a slender but surprisingly strong hand to the rancher. "Beth, haven't seen you in a while. How you be?" He bent at the waist penguin-like, and gave her a quick fatherly hug. "Beautiful as ever."

"And who's this lovely young lady visiting with you? Did you adopt one of them fancy New York City girls when I wasn't paying attention? Couldn't possibly be Kate Flannery. Every time I see Kate Flannery she's got a book in front of her face. Now I think about it I haven't really seen her face since you brought her home from the hospital three days after she was born. Really didn't know for sure if she had a face or not." He gave Kate's braid a church bell-ringer's tug.

Like most of the ranchers in the county, Dave harbored the utmost respect and affection for Doctor Walters. For over forty-five years the vet had saved the lives of countless cattle, sheep, horses, goats, dogs, and cats in all kinds of weather, at all hours of the day and night.

"Good to see you, Doc. How's Mary?"

"She's good. She baked a peach pie this morning, that's how good she be. Can't wait to get home, matter of fact. Might skip dinner and just have a piece of pie or two. Dollop of vanilla ice cream on top, too. What brings you in, Dave?"

"Well, we got us a hurt bird. Ain't no canary neither. Pretty good-sized hawk of some kind. Don't know if it's a boy or a girl, but somehow it slammed into the side of our house about an hour ago and banged up its leg. These two lady friends of mine decided we should come to town to see if you can save him."

"Well, bring it in. Let's have us a gander. Mary's already gone home for the day, so Kate will have to be my assistant. You don't mind a little blood and gore splashing about here and there do you, Kate?" He smiled puckishly. "Do you have a hood on him?"

Dave looked helplessly at his wife and daughter. "A hood?"

"Dad," Kate said, "I think people who train falcons or hunting birds, put small black hoods over the bird's eyes to keep it calm or something." She gazed expectantly up at Doc Walters.

"Exactly right, Kate. I knew all your reading would pay off. You'll make a mighty good vet some day. You best hurry up though, cause one of these years I'm gonna be too danged old for this job." He rubbed one hand through his thin white hair. "Birds are a skittish lot when you move 'em around, Dave, so like Kate says, most trainers keep 'em shackled and hooded. But since he hasn't flown away by now he must have a serious wing or leg problem. Hawks are clever and he's figured out by now, you mean him no harm."

A few minutes later Orville was resting on his back staring up at four humans and a very bright light. Doc Walters had put on a pair of thickly padded gloves and was gently examining Orville. "Well, no need for an x-ray. Anybody can see his leg is broken. He's a male red-tailed hawk by the way. The red-tails have exquisite vision, and they're the best hunters in South Dakota. Something strange about this particular bird though."

"What's that?" Kate asked. She peered curiously at Orville.

"Don't know exactly, but his eyes aren't quite right. I've never been this close to a live hawk before, but his eyes aren't structured like any of my textbook pictures. Might explain why he flew into something as big as your house. He's not blind, but he may not see as well as he should." The doctor shrugged his shoulders. "This guy's eyes seem a little bigger and rounder than they should be. Another anomaly." He paused, his eyebrows lifted and the wrinkles in his forehead deepened. "Kate, anomaly?"

Kate's eye's shuttered for an instant, her brain sifting through thousands of pages of words in less time than it would have taken to tap the word anomaly into her iPad mini for a Google search—"I think anomaly means something different or unexpected."

"Indeed it does," Doc Walters said. "Can't fool this girl with my fancy doctor lingo anymore. Another anomaly is this hawk's eye sockets should be slanted slightly downward, but his straight stare is like two clocks on a wall. Evolution, no doubt, constructed a hawk's eyes tilted downward so it can monitor the ground more efficiently during the hunt, a definite advantage in survival. Something apparently went haywire in this case." He rubbed his forehead thoughtfully with the tips of his glove.

"Tell you one thing though. I'm almost afraid to fix his leg. Hawks hunt by slamming into whatever they're after, and I'm not sure a repaired leg even if it heals properly—a mighty big if—will stand up to those brutal, high speed collisions." The doctor glanced at his young assistant. "Might be best to do him a favor and put him to sleep forever." He sighed and rubbed his gloved hand over Orville's head. "He's a gorgeous bird, ain't he?"

Dave spoke first. "Whatever you think is best, Doc. No sense in letting him suffer or die of starvation just 'cause he can't hunt no more." He turned to Kate and Beth. "What do you say, girls?"

Kate flinched. Her eyes flashed stubborn. "I think we should try to fix his leg. Gramma and I will care for him until he can fly away. He won't be any trouble at all, will he, Mom?"

"I agree with you, Kate, and I know Gramma would love to help care for him too, but Dr. Walters deals with these kinds of issues every day, and he knows best, honey. If he thinks the hawk should be put to sleep, then..." Beth's eyes became deep pools as she gazed down at Orville.

"When I graduated vet school, down to Omaha, Kate, I was twenty-two years old, and I didn't really understand what death means. I held the young man's common notion, based mostly on ignorance and inexperience, that life goes on forever, and I could and should cure all animal health problems. Turned out, I was way wrong. Took me a couple years to get it straight in my head, but eventually I realized some things either can't be fixed or are better not fixed. This bird here is just as important to me as one of your father's steers, and I'm thinkin'..."

Doc Walters's eyes blinked rapidly and he turned his head for a long moment to stare at something invisible out the small window. "Tell you what, young Kate Flannery. We might be able to save him if you and your gramma are willing to nurse him back to health." He wiped his nose on the back of his gloved hand. "He'll need to be fed four or five times a day, and given plenty of fresh water. Gradually, as his strength builds, he'll need to be exercised, too. Will you promise me you'll care for him like he's your best friend?"

Kate grinned at Doc Walters. "I promise. I'll take really, really good care of him."

"Will you shake on it?" He extended his hand toward Kate and she folded her small hand into his. "Fine then, it's decided. It'll be at least six weeks until he regains enough power to hunt properly. I'll charge you twenty dollars, Dave, to cover the cost of the anesthetic and the cast." He grinned broadly. "And, I'll pay Kate twenty dollars for being my assistant. What do you say?"

"Of course," Beth said. "Kate and Gramma will look after him." She put an arm around her daughter's shoulders.

"Sounds good to me," Dave said. "Thanks, Doc."

"Okay then, the account is settled," Doc Walters said. "The tax man don't need to know nothing about this little transaction. I'll put the hawk to sleep with a whiff of oxygen and isoflurane, and then cast him up. Never doctored much on birds before, so this should be fun. Once he's nodded off I'll check his wings too, but they appear fine from here."

An hour later, Dave, Beth, and Kate Flannery pulled out of the Dupree Dairy Queen drive-through with four vanilla cones and a semi-conscious red-tailed hawk. Four blocks later, Kate hopped out and hurried a rapidly melting cone into Doc Walter's office.

Back in the truck, like a preening cat cleaning its soiled paws, she licked a sticky smudge of ice cream off the side of her hand. "Doc said, 'Thanks for the cone and for saving the hawk.'"

"Old Doc's a good man," Beth said. "Typical South Dakota. Always willing to help and never expecting a dime for it."

The intense pain in Orville's leg had lessened considerably, making the ride back to the ranch a whole lot more tolerable. *Interesting day so far*, he thought. *Wonder why I didn't get one of those ice cream cones? If anyone deserves a treat you'd think it'd be the hawk with the broken leg.* Moments later, his heavy eyes drooped against the blinding sun, and he let the vibration of the Ford's tires on Highway 212, headed west back toward Red Elm, lull him sound asleep.

Chapter Five
School of Flight

THE VERY FIRST TIME HIGGINS LAID EYES ON RT Orville Hampstead he knew Orville would be something special. Higgins had spent a sleepless night, his mind reeling with flashing images of flying mechanics, attack manuals, geometry formulas, terrain and predator recognition drills, and wing strength exercises.

As usual, school took up exactly one hour after dawn Monday through Friday in the old Bailey barn out along Thunder Butte creek. On Saturday mornings until noon, the students would fly practice takeoffs, landings, and various swoop formations. Every Sunday morning they flew the eighty miles, as a hawk flies, in tight formation from Iron Lightning to the capitol building over in Pierre at 500 East Capitol Avenue to see the magnificent bronze memorial sculpture, The Fighting Stallions.

Higgins wanted his students to be inspired by it and to understand how precious life is, so they'd never think of wasting their own, nor the life of any living creature.

After a brief rest in a splendid pair of nearby oak trees, on Higgins's signal, the class would accelerate up to the majestic capitol dome, chest bump one pigeon each, just to let those smart-aleck city birds know a proud band of country hawks was visiting, and then it was a mad dash back to the school. The race was on!

Higgins lumbered along, mostly sightseeing, miles behind the fledglings, like the slow old bird he was. Usually the race back was between Amelia, long-winged Johnny, or Lindy, but once in a while, Armstrong or Sally would zoom in and alight atop the school flagpole first for the victory. Even though there was no prize for the winner, the youngsters loved the competition each week; and without realizing it, their navigation and hunting skills were developing along with the improved endurance and wing strength produced by sustained effort.

Old Farmer Bailey had passed away years ago, and his wife, unable to run the farm by herself or sell it, had abandoned ship and moved to Seattle to be close to her son, who preferred peddling cups of coffee at Starbucks to farming his dad's and grandpa's hard won South Dakota land.

Eventually the Iron Lightning hawk community, led by the local Chamber of Commerce, assumed the Bailey property and built thirty perches, two restrooms, a cafeteria, a gym, a state of the art weight room, a modest library, and an administrative office inside an unwanted, falling down Bailey barn. Sure, it wasn't the prettiest school ever built, but it suited the young hawks, and more importantly, their parents and the other local taxpayers just fine.

One early September morning, at eight o'clock sharp, Higgins's chest puffed out and he called roll, "Gus, Tobi, Wilbur, Amber, Frank, Harper..." He had been taught years before, up in Pierre, to arrange the students on their perches male, female, male, female to avoid as much unnecessary male to male and female to female gabbing as possible.

Young hawks, like most adolescent creatures, are more reserved when they are around members of the opposite sex. In the proper place, at the proper time, there's nothing wrong with a bit of giddy fledgling horseplay or chatting, but in the classroom a teacher needs one hundred percent student focus if he expects one hundred percent results. Higgins expected, demanded, and received nothing else. Also, once a month, parent-chaperoned "Talon Hop" dances were held in the cafeteria, when the students could strut the male to female booty thing, if they cared to, until midnight.

In the classroom Higgins was perched six feet below his students, in the traditional hawk system. They were arranged in first name alphabetical, male/female order on stair-stepped perches, allowing Higgins to see the back row of students easily. The staggered arrangement forced the students to gaze down at their teacher and the blackboard at the exact angle their heads would normally be at the moment of attack.

Of course, by the end of the school day, Higgins's neck was exhausted from gazing up at them all day long; but to a dedicated teacher a tired neck is a small price to pay for excellence in the classroom. Higgins was totally committed to his craft, and refused to accept anything but full attention and effort from his students. He admitted candidly, without hesitation, that many a young hawk suffered mild embarrassment under his glare, from a sharp word, or worse yet, a quick snap of his wingtip for not being devoted completely to the lesson at hand.

Higgins was not then, nor was he ever a mean-spirited teacher. His friends and family actually considered him softhearted to a fault, but his persona in the classroom, out of need, was deliberately stern, business-like, and if need be, icy cold. He loved his students, but he had been taught, and wholeheartedly believed, a teacher's showy outward affection does not produce exceptional flyers.

And so he deliberately remained aloof until after their graduation when his teaching was done. In their yearbooks, on graduation day, he always wrote in his distinctive and elegant style: *Your flight instructor once, but now, a friend, forevermore. RT Boyd Higgins.*

Mathematics does not come naturally to hawks, but it is essential for them to master algebra, geometry, and the various angle computations occurring at lightning-like speed in the mind of an attacking hawk. A casual observer, seated in the shade and comfort of a porch rocker, sipping iced lemonade on a scorching South Dakota afternoon, might notice a hawk dropping like a stone seemingly out of nowhere onto a plowed field after a mouse hiding in a furrow, and think little of it. But, the mathematical computations made in an attacking hawk's brain during its unerring descent, make the Roman arch or a lethal chess gambit, algebraic child's play.

And so, Higgins presented mathematics. They began, as all students must, with simple addition, subtraction, division, and multiplication. The class learned how to manipulate, stack, toss—and sometimes, even, juggle numbers. When things became too complicated—too frustrating—too confusing, the young hawks screeched aloud, "Kiiikeeri!" *Somebody, I beg of you, help me!*

From the very first day, Orville had stood out. His wing flailed the air almost before the questions escaped his teacher's beak. "Higgins, sir," he cried out, "I believe seventeen times two equals thirty-four."

Almost before Higgins could utter his pleased agreement, "Indeed it is, young fellow," Orville continued his explanation.

"Therefore, it follows, Higgins, sir, thirty-four divided in half, must be seventeen." Orville's eyes, although wrenched a bit out of shape, smoldered with the same raging intellectual curiosity and intensity distinguishing a red-tailed hawk's eyes from all other birds. "To be able to recognize mathematical patterns is a precious gift," Orville added, his voice trembling with earnest innocence.

"Bravo, lad," Higgins replied. "You've built your nest in a strong tree indeed." Higgins studied each student, searching for faces lacking certainty with what had just been said.

"Now, let's give someone else a chance." Still unfamiliar with their names, he glanced down at his perching chart. "What say you about Orville's declarations, Annabelle?"

Her name stood out in his mind because he was troubled by a note placed in her student file the previous year by her junior high teacher: *Annabelle is a wonderful young hawk, but she lacks the self-confidence necessary to become a top-flight huntress. I worry she will not take the fight to the prey.*

"Higgins, sir..." Annabelle faltered. "Everyone knows Orville is ever so smart, and I wouldn't dare contradict him." Her wings fluttered nervously.

"Annabelle," Higgins said, rather sharply, "Orville's answers, in this instance, are one hundred percent correct; but your mind is also razor-edged, every bit as finely honed as his."

Higgins softened his tone. His eyes never left her face. "If Orville should ever be incorrect, what then?" He lifted his shoulders and let his wings extend fully. "I expect, nay, I demand Annabelle, you must contradict him if you suspect he's wrong. We hawks, like all living creatures, do make mistakes, and sometimes errors lead us straight to the doorstep of tragedy. Consider this: if you and Orville are flying risky business together on a mission someday, and Orville miscalculates, it could cost you both your lives if you don't challenge him."

Higgins slowly shifted his gaze from face to face, letting his words sink in. "We must work in concert, in school and out, one for all and all for one. We are in school today for one reason, and one reason only, to prepare ourselves for the future. We do not gather here to brag about, nor admire, nor place on a pedestal our shining stars. Our daily work together will springboard all of you into becoming the finest hunters South Dakota has ever seen. We have been given much: clear vision, strong wings, deep courage. We must not waste our precious gifts." He paused, leaving the classroom in utter silence until the ticking clock on the wall made its presence known. "Do I make myself clear?"

Orville and twenty-nine other young hawks—perhaps Annabelle's voice the strongest of all—answered in unison, "Indeed, Higgins, sir."

It was then RT Boyd Higgins realized this year's crop of young red-tails were an extraordinary group, and frankly, he was almost insane with happiness. He really was.

Chapter Six

Rhyme, Rhythm, and History

KATE WOKE SHORTLY AFTER DAWN. NEXT TO HER bed, on the nightstand usually reserved for books, Orville slept, still ensconced in the laundry basket. She quietly slipped out from under the covers and stood for a moment peering into Orville's nest. Satisfied her patient was safely breathing, she padded lightly out of her room to the hall bathroom. She quickly showered, and then dressed in light blue shorts and matching sleeveless top. Downstairs in the kitchen, she slid onto the polished smooth wooden bench seat of the family kitchen nook next to her father.

Across the table sat Dave's mother, seventy-eight-year-old Gramma Flannery. She offered a cheerful, "Good morning, Katie Sue. It's a fine day. Are you?"

As a young and beautiful career girl, Gramma had taught English in a Chicago junior high school until she met the equally young and ruggedly handsome Ernie Flannery who had been yanked out of South Dakota to help fight World War II. All these years later, she still loved playing with the sounds of words and wrote, almost daily, "home pomes" as she called them.

"Fine as wine, Gramma mine," Kate volleyed across the table. Whenever Gramma Flannery pitched rhymes at her, Kate tried to respond in kind, and often go one better.

Dave grunted like a sleepy bear being disturbed from a winter nap. "Morning, Kate." His voice sounded thick and he didn't look up from the morning *Rapid City Journal.* "How's the bird?" He folded the newspaper in half and placed it beside his empty plate, smoothing it out with his big hands.

Beth had prepared a breakfast of French toast and bacon. Dave had already finished eating when Kate arrived; he was slowly sipping his second cup of black coffee.

"He's still asleep, I think. I read out loud to him until a little after ten and he never moved once. He kept staring at me, and every time I turned a page his eyes blinked, almost like he was reading along with me. I remember in kindergarten when I was just learning how to read, Ms. Fuller would read to us every morning and I would watch her just like he watched me last night."

Gramma waded a small piece of French toast through an amber pool of maple syrup with her fork. "Mean to say, your bird is a nerd?" She delicately hoisted the bite to her mouth, popped it in, and thoughtfully chewed.

Kate giggled, sipped her orange juice, paused a moment and then replied, "Rest assured, he knows a word." A light dusting of rusty freckles wrinkled atop her carefully chiseled nose. "He's a hawk who likes to gawk."

"Stop that silly talk, you two," Beth said from across the room. "Kate, do you want one or two pieces of bacon?"

Kate bumped her dad with an elbow. "Two will do, but I won't shun one."

She batted her eyelashes innocently across the table at Gramma Flannery who almost choked on a swallow of coffee.

Dave turned toward his daughter, reached out two massive arms, and put her in a gentle headlock. "You're driving your mom crazy with rhyming." He released her, drained his cup with a last noisy swig, wiped his mouth on the edge of his hand, and stood. "I'm gonna be fixing a busted fence out along the west border by Swanson's hollow this morning. Who wants to come along?" He glanced hopefully at his wife.

Beth turned away from the stove and said, "Not I."

"What, you don't want to help me dig some little ol' post holes? Nothin' like jabbing in post holes to take off a pound or two. Better than yoga for losing weight." He smiled broadly at his slim wife who obviously needed no help maintaining her figure.

"I've got two poets to ride herd on, bread to bake, and a whole lotta garden to weed," she said. "You're on your own today, big boy." Her lips puckered and she flew a pretend kiss across the room. "And you'll pay later for that pound or two remark, mister."

"Kate, how about you?"

"I think I'll pass, Dad. I've got a poet, an injured hawk, and a whole lotta mom to keep out of trouble." She picked up her dad's empty coffee cup, slurped a loud pretend swig, then with an exaggerated swipe, wiped her mouth with the side of her hand. "Nothing like a hot cup of joe to jumpstart my day," she said.

Dave laughed at his daughter's mimicry. "I should be home for lunch about noon," he said.

"What do hawks eat, Dad?"

"Not exactly sure. My guess is what they eat have either no legs or very short legs and run real close to the ground. Furry little critters."

"How about worms or peanut butter?"

"Kinda doubt the peanut butter, and I've never seen a hawk down on the ground yanking on a worm like a robin. I'm thinking snakes, lizards, mice, squirrels, and such. I've seen 'em harvest a ring-necked pheasant right out of the air. Your mom has some old leftover venison in the freezer. You could thaw out a chunk and cut up some little bitty pieces for him. Probably do just fine. Don't forget, Doc Walters told you to give him all the fresh water he wants." He leaned down and kissed the top of his daughter's head. "I've gotta get going before it's too hot to work."

To Gramma Flannery he said, "Bye, Mom. Have a grand morning. See you at lunch."

Beth placed a blue platter of bacon and French toast on the table. She wiped her hands on her apron front and said, "Help yourself, Kate. I'm going to walk Dad out to the truck, and then I'll join you for breakfast."

A half hour or so later, Orville awoke flat on his back, his right leg stiffly pointing at the ceiling in Kate's upstairs bedroom. He had a moment of disorientation, and then the events of the previous day flew back into his memory. He could hear human sounds from below. Diffused light streamed through the two windows, heralding another gorgeous South Dakota morning.

Where's what's her face? he thought. He stretched his neck and swiveled his head, but Kate's pillow was empty. He tried opening his wings, but the laundry basket was too confining. He felt lopsided lying on his back with the heavy band of white plaster of Paris cast on his broken leg. *I've got to get out of here.*

He snapped his wings open as far as they'd go and pushed hard with his good left leg against the side of the basket. Just as it tipped over, and he tumbled harmlessly out onto a colorfully braided oval shaped bedside rug, Kate bounced into the room.

"Good morning," she said cheerfully. "I see you're up and about. Try to be a little more careful about falling out of bed, will you? It's important not to bang your bad leg up again."

The girl knelt down next to him on the floor. "I'm glad you're awake. I trust you've slept well. Let's go downstairs and get you some breakfast."

She scooped up Orville and carried him down to the kitchen cradled gingerly in her arms like a newborn infant. Gramma and Beth were washing and drying the morning dishes side by side in front of the big sink.

"May I feed that left-over piece of bacon to our hawk, Mom?"

The two women turned around and stared. "Our hawk?" Beth said. "I don't think he belongs to us, Kate.

If he belongs to anyone he belongs to the sky. He'll soon fly away so don't get too attached to him." Wiping her soapy hands on a towel she stepped toward them and added, "Sure. Give him the bacon, and there's one more piece of French toast on the stove, too."

"Is he meek with his beak?" Gramma asked. "Oh, dear Kate, do be careful; wild things are so unpredictable."

"I'm not sure how or why," Kate replied, "but I trust he won't fly. No reason for alarm; I'm quite certain he won't do me any harm." She took a paper napkin off the counter and using it as a glove picked up the bacon and French toast. "We'll sit under the apple tree, a cool place to read a story." Kate flipped the words over her shoulder as she glided out the back door.

She placed Orville on the army blanket and held out a small chunk of crisp bacon. His green gold eyes met her blues, blinked once, twice, and then he opened his beak and gently snatched the bacon from her fingers. The bite disappeared, his eyes blinked, and a soft, "Trrrr" Thank you, dear friend, fled from his throat.

Kate, sensing Orville's appreciation, giggled. "You're welcome, little buddy. Mom makes great breakfasts." She offered another piece of bacon, which was quickly accepted and consumed. Then she tore the slice of French toast into hawk-sized bites and offered them to him one by one. A moment later when the last piece had been gulped down, she said, "I'm going to get you something to drink."

She soon returned with a plastic Tupperware container of cold water.

Orville blinked his eyes. "Trrrr," he said, his ruffled head swiveling toward the Tupperware.

She placed the water dish in front of him and he drank, tipping his head back to swallow. "Trrrr," he repeated, when finished drinking.

"Wow! You were thirsty."

Kate, like all South Dakota girls, had her morning chores to complete before she could relax for the day. Leaving Orville alone on the blanket to ponder his current situation as an invalid under her care, she raced upstairs, made her bed, brushed her teeth, and tidied up the bathroom towels and sink; next she carried yesterday's dirty clothes to the small laundry room, popped the washer door open, and pushed in a rumpled load of whites, added soap, and started the wash cycle; almost done, she grabbed the broom and dustpan from behind the door.

Back at the apple tree, she caught Orville napping, a bit of drool clinging to the side of his beak. "Hey, lazy bones," she said, "Wake up. I've got a bit more work to do and then we'll take a walk. Mom's number one rule is: 'A clean house is a happy house.' Her second rule is: 'Work until done, then play.' You wait here. I'll be back in a jiffy."

Quickly she swept the rarely used front porch, and then the back porch where all the daily traffic entered the kitchen. Next she found a white cloth in the ragbag, grabbed the bottle of blue Windex off the shelf, and sprayed the windshield and windows of the family Toyota, making sure to scrub the sun-baked bugs off the headlights, and to polish the dust-covered taillights.

After putting away her cleaning materials, she cartwheeled herself back to Orville's make-shift hospital bed under the shady comfort of the apple tree.

Orville amused himself by watching the tree's leaves flutter in the morning breeze. On any ordinary day, Orville would have been six hundred and fifty feet aloft, scanning the prairie below for the slightest movement. Today, lying on his back aboard an old tattered army blanket, he reversed the routine, scanning the universe instead. He quickly discovered once past the tree there's little movement in the deep blue void beyond. Not counting the colonies of puffy white wind-blown clouds scampering about, of course.

"I'm almost done," Kate announced. "My last chore this morning is to walk out to the road and get the mail." Without waiting for Orville's agreement, she hoisted him into her arms and started down the long narrow driveway leading toward the main road out of the ranch.

"Dad says it's like a half mile to the mailbox, but most days it seems lots farther."

She held Orville up to her face so she could make direct eye contact. As they walked along she freely shared her ancestry, not so much out of pride, but rather an honest need to share in friendship.

"My great-grampa Ulis Flannery homesteaded here, and my grampa Ernie, who died two years ago, inherited the land from him. My dad's name is Dave Flannery and he raises six hundred head of Red Angus cattle here now. Originally, Black and Red Angus registered cattle came to America from Scotland. Most ranchers these days prefer the black, but my grampa Ernie thought the red tolerate the heat better here in South Dakota, so he bought a hundred head over in Wyoming just after he came home from the war—1946 or '47 I think it was. My teacher said America won the war, but personally I don't think anybody really wins if sixty million people have to be killed before somebody decides it's over."

She carefully shifted Orville to her other arm before continuing her narrative. "Anyway, my dad's mom, Susan, whom we call Gramma, and my mom, Beth, live here too. Mom takes care of us and besides being a great mom she's also a successful pen and ink artist. She sells some of her drawings at county fairs and even at Wall Drug. I don't know if you've heard of Wall Drug or not, but it's a kind of famous tourist place not too far from here, just off the freeway. She'll most likely want to make a pencil sketch of you in a day or two when you feel up to it. Or maybe she'll use charcoal.

"Gramma Susan grew up in Chicago. She's a big-time Cubs baseball fan and poet. Some of her poems have been published in the newspaper and a couple of magazines. She wrote a kinda famous one called 'South Dakota Suffering.' I guess a lot of people like it.

"My name is Kate. Well, Katherine Susan Flannery officially. I was born down in Philip twelve years, eleven months, and sixteen days ago. I'll turn thirteen September tenth. In case you're not familiar with calendars that's just a couple more weeks. I like to read, fish, and swim. At school I play volleyball and softball. I'm not popular or anything though because some of the kids think I like school too much."

Kate paused and her eyes closed for the barest of moments as if her private revelation somehow stung. She rubbed a slim forefinger under her nose to blot a pooling drip, and then with no further hesitation, continued.

"Actually I think it's impossible to like school too much. If you want to know the real truth, little buddy, I love school. But, I'm not particularly fond of broccoli and, like I said, I abhor war; I also pretty much detest the New York Yankees. They think it's perfectly okay to buy all the best players just so they can win the World Series every year. Their attitude really stinks. I want to be a veterinarian, a writer, or a librarian when I grow up. Since I don't have a brother though, I may end up as a rancher when Dad gets too old to run our acreage. Ranching is in our blood. And you are?"

Orville had remained silent during Kate's lengthy family history lesson and her pointed editorial on war and baseball; but nonetheless he appeared keenly interested, taking it all in, politely bobbing his head in acknowledgement and understanding. Orville clearly understood Kate was introducing herself and her family to him, and when she stopped talking, he tried his best to respond to her last question appropriately.

He opened his beak, blinked his eyes, and a sound remarkably close to Oorrvuul flowed out. *Hunting is my family blood.*

He also intended to share something of his own life and family as is customary for red-tails when introduced to a stranger. Of course, he also wanted to inquire about what Kate might want for her thirteenth birthday gift; ask if Gramma Susan had ever written any hawk poems; explain his own position on war and the Yankees; and find out what her mother's third rule might be.

He also found it extremely curious that an intelligent, kind, pretty, and cheerful young girl wouldn't be popular with her classmates, but before he could translate his thoughts into understandable English, Kate interrupted him.

"Did you just say 'Orville'? And your family are hunters? What a cool name. In third grade I did a book report on the Wright brothers, Orville and Wilbur, who made the first sustained human flight in 1903. Of course you probably know a lot more about flying than they did."

Orville, well aware of the Wright brothers' accomplishments, managed a wry smile. But he was much more interested in Kate's other issues, and for the time being decided to keep his personal thoughts on the invention of flying machines to himself.

Having finally arrived at the end of the driveway, Kate reached up, opened the mailbox door, peered inside, and grabbed a handful of envelopes. "Just bills, Orvie." She thumbed quickly through the mail. "Nothing for you."

Orville's self-introduction and Kate's issues, presumably, were revealed on the stroll back up the half-mile long dusty driveway to the Flannery home where he and Kate had first met just one day earlier.

Chapter Seven
Two More Creeks

WORLD WAR II PILOTS—THE GERMANS, JAPAnese, Brits, and Yanks—sometimes became lost in the fog, especially over unfamiliar territory. Their disorientation often resulted in an empty fuel tank, ditching at sea, or a devastating land crash. Radar, still in the early stages of development, was not completely reliable.

Nowadays, with global positioning satellites and other sophisticated electronic systems, pilot navigation is virtually foolproof. However, a hawk's brain today is wired exactly the same as his great-grandfather's brain was all those years ago during the war. Hence a vigilant hawk, must permanently engrave in his mind the territory below him each and every day he flies. A keen sense of local geography—lakes, rivers, creeks, ravines, canyons, and buttes—all the places where potential game make their home, is absolutely essential, lifesaving knowledge for young hawks.

Many a disoriented hawk, blinded by wind-driven prairie dust has ended up weak and helpless clear over in Wyoming because of poor navigational skills. Just last winter, two Iron Mountain hawks were lost to the cruel fury of a wandering North Dakota blizzard; eyes frozen shut, they slammed into Rattlesnake Butte, and were buried in snow. They suffocated before a rescue squad could locate them.

A slow smile creased Boyd Higgins's face as he drilled the class during a morning review to prepare the students for their final geography test. He fired his questions, bang, bang, and he expected instant and specific answers.

"Sally, please name all the Ziebach County creeks still flowing in late summer before I count to ten."

"Worthless, Ruddy, Red Scaffold, Moreau, Thunder Butte, Irish, Girl, Luis, Flint Rock, Sophie, Mud, Felix, and Straight Head creeks, Higgins, sir," replied Sally without the slightest hesitation.

Sally was one of Higgins's favorite students, though he did his best to conceal it. Anyone who has ever perched in a classroom with a teacher who plays favorites has seen the dark shadow of resentment flutter by on ugly wings.

Sally fluffed her tail feathers and smiled confidently down at Higgins on his perch just below the blackboard. A hawk's smile definitely takes some getting used to. Nature has cemented a constant grim glare on a red-tail's countenance, but in truth, along with Airedale Terriers, red-tailed hawks are among the happiest of earth's creatures. Sally presented Higgins with a confident and sugary smile.

He returned a sour-faced scowl. Surprised and truly disappointed, he asked, "Have you forgotten one glistening ribbon of blue water somewhere, young fledgling?" His voice wobbled, revealing his disappointment. "Have we flown east, north, south, and west every Monday morning for the past nine months for nothing?"

Despair is an almost unknown emotion for hawks, but for the first time since September, something akin to it clutched Higgins's heart. On the very eve of Sally's graduation had he somehow failed his student? How could Sally not know, even in her sleep, every precise detail of their practice hunting grounds?

Reluctantly, Higgins pointed a wingtip at Orville. "Help your classmate out, lad."

Orville blinked his eerie eyes solemnly and said, without a smidgen of smugness, "I believe my esteemed classmate, Sally, has overlooked Red Earth Creek, due northeast of here. It harbors the largest colony of white-tail rabbits in the state, Higgins, sir."

Once you've peered deep into Orville's eyes you'll never forget their green-gold color, intense black pupils, and rather odd shape. "Surely there is more concerning our vital hunting ground, Orville. Is that all you've learned in the past thirty-six weeks?"

"Oh no, Higgins, sir. Red Earth Creek flows southeast until it joins Worthless Creek just north of the town of Green Grass in Dewey County. The water's depth and flow rate—"

"Thank you, Orville. Quite enough. Such basic information, locked forever in your brain, may someday prove vital to your very survival."

Higgins glanced up at Sally. He could see the hurt in her eyes. Gently, he said, "Sally, what else can you tell us about Red Earth Creek?"

She tensed on her perch. "Higgins, sir, a momentary lapse. I beg the class to forgive me."

Boyd Higgins wanted to wrap his wings around her, knowing full well the depth of her embarrassment at making such an elementary mistake.

Instead, he said, "Sally, we hawks are not computers. We are flyers. We do make mistakes. But by educating ourselves we are able to minimize the results of our errors and prevent disasters. Many years ago, when I was still very young and incredibly handsome, I myself misjudged the power of a Canadian Bald Eagle one foggy morning, and was quite fortunate to escape with my life. Please continue, Sally."

Higgins's self-aggrandizing humor diffused the situation. After the class finished hooting about his "incredibly handsome" comment, Sally flashed a smile and said, "Even in late August we still find sufficient water there to sustain us and those we hunt. Orville was absolutely correct in his other statements." Speaking confidently now, she continued, "Flying over Red Earth Creek at attack altitude we can easily see in great abundance—"

"That will do, Sally," Higgins interrupted. "Class, the state ophthalmologist from Pierre will be here at ten this morning to administer your mandatory eye examinations. Each of you passed the preliminary eye exam last September to be admitted to flight school, but that rudimentary test just established the fact you can see well enough to fly without endangering yourself or others. Today's test is the real deal." He paused momentarily.

"After the vision exam, promptly at eleven o'clock, all students will report to the gym for wing strength measurements. Then at eleven-thirty sharp you will take your final math, geography, and language tests in Bailey Hall. Finally, at five o'clock this evening we will celebrate together the conclusion of your schooling with the Wings Aloft graduation banquet and awards ceremony in the cafeteria with your families."

After guiding these young hawks every day for nine months, Higgins, overwhelmed with their accomplishments, allowed himself a moment of pride. They had bravely faced and surpassed all of his challenges and proved to be even better students than he had ever dreamed they could be. And he, blessed to be the lighter of the fire, the firm hand gripping the tiller, the soft touch on the potter's wheel—their teacher, drowned in emotion.

Speechless, he allowed his eyes to roam the classroom, momentarily touching each of theirs. Hawks communicate so much of their feelings through direct eye contact. The students' eyes, mirrors to his own, responded—glistening and overflowing with the joy and well-deserved pride of successfully completing flight school. They had given themselves freely to him and he had shaped them into the state's finest young flyers.

Higgins finally broke the silence. "If any of you, for any reason whatsoever, fail the eye exam, the strength test, or any of your written tests, you will not be allowed to graduate with the others." He paused for emphasis.

"We have worked tremendously hard, and now it is up to you to perform to your individual potential." He hoped the tears forming in the corners of his eyes were unseen. What a bloody fool he was! Nothing is invisible to a South Dakota red-tail. There was a deep lump in his throat and his eyes blinked rapidly.

"The bar has been set exceptionally high, but I have complete faith in your ability. Any questions?"

As one heart and one voice, they shouted, "Indeed not, Higgins, sir. We are ready!"

The majesty of their youth overwhelmed him then, and he quickly turned his back so they would not see two more shallow and somewhat salty un-named creeks flowing uninterrupted down his feathery cheeks.

Chapter Eight
Ancient Animosity

Three days had gone by since Orville's flying mishap. So far his injured leg seemed to be healing up nicely and Kate, as she had promised Dr. Walters, tended to Orville as if he were her best friend. In fact, they quickly had become nearly inseparable.

After depositing the morning mail on the kitchen table, as she did six days a week, Kate carried Orville out to her favored place under the apple tree. The portable radio she kept there had a large round plastic handle about fifteen inches long and perhaps an inch in diameter.

"Orville, as far as I can tell, except for this broken leg, you're perfectly fine and you should be able to stand on your good leg."

She tenderly held Orville above the radio's handle with two hands. He instinctively lowered his left leg and grasped the handle as he might perch upon a tree branch. His cast enclosed right leg jutted stiffly out to the side. When Kate removed her grip, he instantly snapped his wings open.

"Don't fly," she cried out, startled by Orville's sudden movement.

Now balanced, he clinched his wings tight to his body and sat statue still, appearing somewhat like a bemused pink flamingo napping in a shallow pond.

"Good boy. Standing on one leg is better for you than lying on the blanket all day. Dr. Walters said to start your physical therapy as soon as possible."

Gramma Flannery, her long gray hair and yellow dress billowing in the morning breeze, came around the corner. She carried a battered old pie tin. On it she had chopped up a piece of venison from last fall's deer hunt.

Orville swiveled his head, blinked his eyes several times in succession, and then, wings folded, hopped off his perch, landing like the infamous pirate Long John Silver on his one good leg. "Trrrr," he murmured politely.

"I've never known a hawk to balk when it comes to talk," Gramma said with a soft laugh. Bending down, she placed the pie tin on the blanket in front of Orville. "Better to eat a deer, than go hungry, my dear." She stepped back.

Orville instantly snatched a piece of meat and swallowed it whole. "Trrrr."

In less than a minute the tin was empty. Orville took two giant, "Mother, may I?" hopscotch type one-legged hops to his water dish and drank heartily. Tipping his beak up toward Kate and Gramma, he tried his best to smile, but as mentioned earlier, a hawk's smile takes some getting used to. Nonetheless, his eyes sparkled like sun-dazzled water on the Moreau River, and anyone in the hawk community would have instantly recognized his grateful countenance as a charmingly handsome grin.

"No rhyme or reason why, but he's a friendly little guy," Gramma said.

Orville stretched his wings and tail feathers wide; he snatched the pie tin in his beak, and in one instant was airborne. He circled Gramma once and then hovering, wings beating the air furiously, held the empty tin out to her.

"Ever so sweet," Gramma said, reaching out and taking the tin, "nice and neat." She rhythmically beat the tin tambourine-like against her thigh. "Sure love this apple tree," she murmured. She spread her arms wide and embraced the rough skinned tree trunk. "Oh, how you comfort me."

As Gramma turned back toward the house Orville settled softly on his radio perch, turned his head toward Kate, and blinked his eyes.

"I think Gramma likes you, Orville. If not now, she no doubt, soon will."

Kate sometimes found herself rhyming even when she didn't intend to.

The next hour sped by as Kate, lying on her back next to Orville on his perch, read out loud to him. Since she had already polished off the seventh grade Suggested Summer Reading List and all of the town librarian's test-drive books, she had re-discovered her cherished copy of *The Hobbit* Gramma had given her last year as a birthday gift.

The book was a bit dog-eared and a few pages sported mustard stains, but Orville didn't seem to mind, listening intently to each word. Although, when Kate read about Gandalf, Bilbo Baggins, and the dwarves being trapped in the burning trees with the wolves leaping and snapping below them, Orville became agitated, opening and closing his wings several times in quick succession.

Kate read excitedly how the flames licked upward and the wolves howled with glee while Bilbo and the others scrambled higher and higher in the trees until there was no escape. Just at the most desperate moment, when they were about to be rescued by the noble-hearted Lord of the Eagles and his tribe, Orville let out a piercing screech, "Urrrrkkeeeena! Urrrrkkeeeena!" Lethal bully of the sky!

Beth Flannery came racing around the corner of the house. "What in the world?" she shouted.

"I've got a feeling Orville doesn't like eagles," Kate said. "He's got a real temper when he gets riled."

"Orville? You've named him Orville? Is his last name Wright, perchance?" Beth smiled at her daughter.

"I didn't name him, Mom. He's told me his first name and some other stuff, but I don't know what his last name is yet. He's still kinda shy."

"Well, Orville it is then," Beth replied. "Please come in now, get washed up for lunch, and set the table. Dad should be home any minute. If you like, bring Orville along too." She glanced askance at Orville seated calmly on his radio perch. "If he can behave himself."

Chapter Nine
Bitter Disappointment

HUMANS OCCASIONALLY USE THE RATHER quaint expression "eyes like a hawk" to indicate a human with above average visual ability. Keen sight is such a vital part of being a hawk it's sometimes taken for granted. Simply stated, without it, hawks would be unable to feed their families and would perish. Evolution has brought them to this point, step by step, and without meaning to crow about it, they have the best vision of any flyers in the world.

The human visual ability measurement called 20/20 refers to an arranged pattern of various sized letters a person with "normal" vision can see clearly from a distance of twenty feet. The number on the right increases to a point of 20/200 or greater, which means the person being tested sees at twenty feet what a person with "normal" vision can clearly see at two hundred feet. Twenty/two hundred is also the cutoff point for legal blindness in the United States, of which South Dakota is a part, albeit rather unenthusiastically.

Red-tailed hawks, on the other hand, have a vision rating of about 20/2. They can see from twenty feet what humans can see at two feet. To put it another way, red-tails can see the whiskers on a mouse's face at an altitude of a mile. Eyes like a hawk, indeed!

Dr. RT Bennington and his young assistant, Nurse Nan, had flown in early in the morning and busied themselves arranging their various eye test contraptions. Higgins rather boastfully remarked, "Dr. Bennington, in my twelve years here at Prairie Winds High not one of my students has failed the state eye exam. Must be the water."

Dr. Bennington, ignoring the teacher's lame attempt at humor, paused with a roll of duct tape he was tearing into strips with his beak and gave Higgins the standard hawk glare.

"Not one hawk in a thousand, nay ten thousand, maybe ten million, ever flunks this test, Boyd," he replied. "Hawks are born with binoculars for eyes, and seldom, if ever, do they fail us. If it weren't for the other birds in this world, I'd be out of a job. Praise be for owls and woodpeckers. I really don't know why the state requires us to conduct these nonsensical tests on hawks. A silly waste of time, right, Nan?"

"I agree, Doctor," she said, "but it does get us out of the office from time to time." She sighed. "And Ziebach County is so beautiful this time of year."

Higgins glanced nervously at his watch and said, "My students will begin lining up for your test, silly waste of time or not, in less than five minutes. Do you want them in first name alphabetical order again this year?"

"If they were a flock of timid chickadees it would make the whole affair go a lot faster," Nan replied. "But with hawks it really doesn't matter. More than likely your fledglings have perfect vision." She flashed a gorgeous hawk smile, and said, "I know, Boyd, what a stickler you are with your students, and I'm guessing you've already instructed them to line up a certain way. Their names are already loaded into my laptop and I can sort their names and enter their scores easily with a simple touch of a button."

The expression "stickler" stung Higgins just a bit, but she was absolutely correct. He was a stickler for details. Predictably, he also always became a bit giddy when around Nurse Nan. After all the time he had spent in the hospital after snapping his wing, he still had a soft spot for health care workers, especially stunningly beautiful ones. As Nurse Nan suspected, he had made a firm point with the students when they arrived at the testing site; they were to line up in first name alphabetical order, with Amelia first and Yancy last.

Dr. Bennington had just completed duct-taping the stuffed carcasses of an ant, a black beetle, a cockroach, a salamander, a garden snake, a field mouse, a Norway rat, a ground squirrel, a hare, and a two-pound walleye to small, square pieces of plywood. Higgins knew from previous years Dr. Bennington and Nurse Nan would then arrange them in a certain pattern on the ground. Most of these creatures are, of course, a hawk's daily prey; and hence, instantly recognizable by any red-tail, worldwide.

The South Dakota hawk vision test, unlike a human visual acuity test, is a timed event. When the signal is given, each of the students will launch off the ground, accelerate quickly to the standard attack level of six hundred and fifty feet, which Higgins will monitor, and cover their left eye first with a black cloth. Then, as Dr. Bennington points to the various objects in the field arrangement with a four-foot length of wooden dowel, the student flyer sings out loudly the name of the object. Nurse Nan simultaneously tallies their responses on her keyboard.

In order to pass the test a student must correctly identify nine of the ten figures with both the left and right eyes. Students who respond correctly for all ten get a special Notation of Visual Excellence on their graduation certificate. In years past, up to ninety-eight percent of Higgins's students had earned the excellence mark. Testing varies slightly from state to state but in South Dakota it must be accomplished in less than one minute.

As instructed, the students promptly flew in and lined up, tail feathers to tummy, behind Amelia, Andy, and Annabelle.

As soon as it was perfectly quiet, Higgins addressed the group. "The timing begins the second your talons leave the ground. At altitude, level off, maintain a tight circle, and watch Dr. Bennington. As he points, you call out in a loud, clear voice the name of the object. When he waves the yellow flag, switch the cloth to your right eye and repeat the process."

Higgins studied their faces. Because of the importance of the test there was a slight trace of nervousness here and there, but no signs of real anxiety.

"When Dr. Bennington waves the white flag, your examination is complete and you will then pass the black cloth to the hawk behind you. Once done, leave the test area immediately and roost quietly in the old poplar tree in front of the gym until all of your classmates have completed the test. Questions?"

Once again Higgins scanned their faces. "Good. Amelia will lead the way, followed by Andy, Annabelle, Brady and so forth. When Yancy is done with his test, we will all regroup in the gym for your wing strength testing."

Nurse Nan, growing weary of Higgins's lengthy instructions, said, "Amelia, please step to the line. I'm going to give Mr. Higgins thirty seconds to get up to his monitoring station, then I'll blow the whistle for you to start."

The entire class burst out laughing at the idea it would take Higgins a full thirty seconds to get his old, creaky carcass airborne and climb to six hundred and fifty feet, something they could negotiate with ease in less than ten seconds.

Higgins had mentioned to his class he had once suffered a severe injury to his wing in a complicated flying maneuver battling an eagle. The fact he couldn't fly for almost six months was bad enough, but it also ultimately cost him his flying career, and threw him head over talons into a severe bout of depression.

At first he was just glad to be alive; many hawks have died in such violent confrontations, but as the physical therapy at the academy hospital in Sioux Falls wore on, it became increasingly difficult for him to maintain his usual upbeat, hopeful attitude.

Girded in a thick leather belt, and suspended in the wind tunnel, simply flapping his wings became a torturous exercise. Some days he was in the pool for hours, swimming against the current until he could barely climb the ladder at the end of the session. Had it not been for Gloria, his physical therapist, he no doubt would have given up and remained a crippled flyer the rest of his days.

Higgins was young and otherwise physically fit then, but if not for Gloria, goading him on each day, it's almost certain he would have remained grounded forever. Gloria, Ms. Easy On The Eyes, and as tough-minded as a marine drill sergeant, saved his life. She forced him to sweat, cry, swear, and hope to die. A year later, the torment over, they flew side by side as hawk and wife.

Forty-five minutes later the testing was complete, and as Yancy flew off to join his classmates in the poplar tree, Higgins glided to a near perfect landing next to Dr. Bennington and Nurse Nan. There was a deep frown on Dr. Bennington's face, no mistake about it.

As Higgins caught his breath, Bennington said, "We have a problem, Boyd."

Higgins glanced sharply at Nurse Nan. The color had drained from her feathers and her face almost matched her cute little nurse's cap. "What is it?" he asked.

"One of your students scored six with the left eye, and four with the right eye. I wouldn't dare grant him flying certification with such poor vision," Dr. Bennington replied. "In the air he is a danger to himself and those he flies with. To be perfectly honest, I don't know how he ever got admitted into flight school."

RT Boyd Higgins's brain reeled; his heart pounded—thunderstruck!

"There must be some mistake," he cried. "There must have been a misunderstanding of the directions." Higgins, his eyes rolling wildly, stared helplessly at Dr. Bennington. "Surely you will retest him?"

"No. I'm not given that option. Our rules are very specific, Boyd," he said.

In a show of empathy he reached out with a wingtip and brushed Higgins's shoulder. "Unless there are severe extenuating circumstances we are not allowed to grant a second test. The test-site weather is crystal clear, the sun is shining brightly, and there is no appreciable wind to kick up dust. There is quite simply, no earthly reason for failure except less than perfect vision, and as you well know, sir, the Temporary Conditional Attack Diploma cannot be granted to any hawk who scores below eighteen of twenty."

Bennington extended his graceful wings, sighed, and said, "I'm very sorry, but the lad scored but nine of twenty. By our standards, he's as blind as a bat. How he got this far along in school is astonishing to say the least. I'm recommending you ground him immediately before he kills himself. I'm quite certain you don't want your student's blood on your hands."

Higgins shuddered at such a dreadful thought; his legs weakened and he felt dizzy for a long moment. Nurse Nan reached out as if to catch him.

"I'm okay," he blurted. Regaining his composure, he said, "What if I petition the superintendent's office up in Pierre for a re-testing?"

"An outside possibility," Dr. Bennington replied, shrugging his shoulders. "It's been tried before once or twice, but to my knowledge, a second test has never been granted."

Higgins, dreading the next question, shifted his gaze between Bennington and the nurse. They both avoided his eyes. His voice quavered. "Who is it?"

Nurse Nan, detecting the emotion in Higgins's voice, stepped forward. Beholding some distant cloud, she whispered, "RT Orville Hampstead."

An icy talon squeezed Higgins's heart. "No," he cried. "It can't be. Not Orville." His world began to spin and go black before he collapsed into Nurse Nan's saving embrace.

Chapter Ten
Caesar and Socrates

KATE AND ORVILLE'S FRIENDSHIP CONTINUED TO blossom, but Kate was disappointed he didn't take the initiative for his own recovery. One morning she said, "Orville I know you have to protect your injured leg, but unless you use your wings frequently the muscles will atrophy and you'll have two medical problems instead of just one. I promised Doc Walters I would see to it you exercise your wings at least twice a day."

Perched on his radio in the shade, Orville bobbed to the beat of an old tune, "I Believe I Can Fly."

Kate sternly interrupted his reverie. "Orville, listen to me. You really need to exercise. Your wing muscles will atrophy if you don't fly. I mean it!"

Orville, taking his inspiration from the music, merely blinked his eyes in response to Kate's suggestion of physical therapy. He truly appreciated Kate's concern, but unknown to her, he could feel the power beginning to surge back into the sinews, tendons, ligaments, and muscles necessary to support heavier than air flight. The nutrition and rest Kate provided him each day had allowed his body to recover from what normally would have been a fatal accident.

And, as a bachelor and somewhat carefree vagabond, he knew his absence from the skies would not alarm his friends or family. It is fairly common for unmarried hawks to wander for days in their search for a mate or fresh hunting grounds. Just last month he'd taken a week off and flew to Wyoming and back merely to see the sights.

In short, Orville was unconcerned about his absence from the sky and confident he would soon completely regain his strength. Meantime he was enjoying his sojourn with the Flannerys and was in no hurry to depart their company.

"I've finished my chores already, Orvie, and I propose we take the rest of the day off for some fishing and swimming over at the river. What do you say? Can you handle it?" Careful not to bump the cast on his broken leg, she picked Orville up and held him at arm's length.

"The river is slightly over a three-mile walk from here. I can't carry you, our lunch, my fishing pole, and the worms. What I need to know is, can you fly there on your own?"

Kate sensed it was a ridiculous, almost insulting question, but she brushed those feelings aside. She was concerned Orville was becoming content to rest in the shade all day. Not lazy exactly, just too laid back to suit her. On the other hand, she didn't want to force him to overstress his wings and set back his recovery.

She lifted Orville about four feet off the ground, placing him on the trunk of the apple tree where it cleaved into two halves. "Do hawks ever catch any fish? My grampa

Ernie showed me a secret pool where channel cats love to nap in the afternoon. If I catch a small one you can have it for your lunch."

For the first time in three days, Orville became truly vibrant. He stretched his wings and fluffed his tail feathers. Remembering his Aquatic Diving class, he could still visualize the list of fish able to survive in a warm water environment like the Moreau River where it flows through Ziebach County.

Higgins had covered the blackboard with rudimentary drawings and forced the class to memorize the common names, the Latin and Greek, and the dorsal shapes of the ten most abundant fish found in the river. Red-tails can easily snatch any fish venturing too close to the surface, but they specialize in channel catfish, blue gill sunfish, and the common carp.

Thrilled at the possibility of sinking his beak into a fat channel cat for his lunch prompted Orville to vocalize, "*Ictalurus punctatus.*" In Latin, fish cat.

Kate giggled. "I have no idea what you just said, but I see that big grin on your face so I guess you're willing to test your wings and tag along with me today. Just in case the fish aren't biting, we've got a bag of chips, two tuna sandwiches, half an apple, some carrot sticks, and two bottles of water. Plenty for both of us, don't you think?"

Gramma Flannery came around the corner carrying Kate's school backpack.

"Everything is sacked and packed. Be wise, youse guys." She sounded more like a New Jersey longshoreman than a South Dakota poet.

Kate, for once, did not boomerang a rhyme back. "Thanks, Gramma. Orville gave me a lesson in Latin or Greek or something just now. I don't know where or how or why he learned it, but he did. Do you think flying to the river and back will be too much for him?"

Orville swiveled his head back to Gramma, and solemnly blinked his eyes twice in rapid succession. He was on the verge of saying, I'm ready to state, Kate, I could fly to the moon soon; but not wanting to be rude he kindly kept his poetic thoughts to himself.

"Keep up a steady gait, Kate. Sing a song; he'll follow along. Feed him a carp or two; fresh fish'll carry him through," said Grandma.

Beth stepped around the corner and said, "Kate, Dad and I are leaving for Rapid City in about an hour. We'll be back home in time for dinner Sunday night. Any special book you want us to get for you?"

"If you can find one, I'd love a good used copy of *To Kill a Mockingbird*. The library at Dupree doesn't have one because someone stole it. Mrs. Koppel says it's a great book for kids like me. One more book should get Orvie and me through the rest of summer vacation."

A kid like me? Beth wondered what exactly the librarian had in mind to say such a thing to Kate. Was it so unusual a South Dakota ranch girl would have an insatiable appetite for books?

A nagging worry for Beth this summer had been the distinct lack of phone calls for Kate. In years past the phone had served as a vital link between Kate and her school chums scattered on isolated farms and ranches for miles around. Had something happened at school to silence these summer vacation friendships? Once or twice Beth had suggested Kate call a friend and have a weekend sleepover, but Kate had dismissed the idea with such an unusual chill in her voice Beth finally dropped the topic for good. After all, why worry about a kid who brought home a report card with straight As and glowing compliments from all her teachers?

She gave Kate a quick hug. "I'm sure we can find one at Paige Turner's, the little bookstore near the motel. Gramma is counting on fried catfish for dinner tonight so you best get going. Be careful, honey. I want you back home from the river no later than five o'clock. Absolutely, leave there no later than four. And let Orville carry something too. He needs the exercise."

"Bye, Mom. Have fun. Tell Dad to get some more black licorice, please. Let's go, Orvie," Kate said. She unzipped her backpack, dropped *The Hobbit* in on top of her lunch, and shrugged the pack's straps over her slender shoulders. Skipping over to the porch, she grabbed her fishing pole and suspended it across two of the clothesline wires.

"Orville, she said, "it's a long walk and I need you to carry my pole. As Grampa Ernie used to say, 'Share the burden to share the bounty.'" Without looking back Kate hiked up the long driveway in the general direction of the river.

Orville sat motionless for a moment longer, watching Kate disappear behind the house. Gramma and Beth waved from the porch. Kate was halfway up the driveway approaching the main road by the mailbox when Orville, without a word of farewell to the women, blinked twice, lifted abruptly from his apple tree perch, and gracefully sailed past them, his injured leg poking oddly out to the side like the kickstand of a parked bicycle.

At the clothesline, he hovered overhead for a moment, and then almost casually, as if it were an everyday event, plucked the fishing pole from the lines with the talons on his good leg, perfectly catching the center balance. He was an ungainly sight with his plaster leg jutting out and an eight-foot fishing rod dangling below, but likewise, a working truck on the South Dakota prairie is not the same shiny, undented beauty on display in the Ford showroom in Sioux Falls either. Life leaves bruises.

Gramma wrapped a thin, sun-freckled arm around her daughter-in-law's shoulders. "Growing up on a ranch without any brothers or sisters is tough on a kid, Beth. I'm glad she loves her books and has Orville to care for. She needs a friend in the worst way."

Beth sighed. "Yes," she said, "but what's going to happen when Orvie leaves her for good? I wish she had more school friends. South Dakota can be such a lonely place."

There was an air of uneasiness in Beth's voice as she turned toward the door. "I've got to pack a few things for the weekend."

Chapter Eleven
A Trusting Heart

THE MOREAU RIVER IN LATE AUGUST IS NOT THE same river it is during spring runoff. Gradually it becomes as lazy and warm as the long days, rolling up its banks and showing off its dirty underwear. Ancient stumps and snags emerge, flaunting their grimy faces; the animals come calling in the night and leave their telltale footprints in the morning mud. It's a meandering, by and by kind of flow, simmered by day, cooled by night.

Kate had been fishing the Moreau ever since her Grampa Ernie took her five-year-old hands in his and taught her how to impale a squirming worm or a fresh-caught grasshopper on a hook. Ever since—like every youngster who's ever waded hip deep into a river and plugged herself into the electric shock of a tugged line, bent pole, and swirling surface water caused by a desperate fish—Kate Flannery had been hooked on fishing.

Even though it had just been a week since his accident, Orville flew swiftly to the river, carefully laid the fishing pole next to the bank, and then circled back to Kate as she trudged along a barely visible rock strewn path north from the ranch house. There were a few remaining scrub shade or fruit trees gone wild along the way. They had been planted in optimism and then neglected by early pioneers who, growing weary of the scalding summer heat and cruel winter cold, had moved on to search out a less hostile place.

Small piles of ash-colored boards lay here and there. These were the decaying artifacts, remnants, where a house had once taken shape, rooted, and become a home; a secure refuge where a strong man and a brave woman became family and budded; where discouragement eventually snuffed the will and chased them forever away. Nature slowly dismantled the boards, but much more quickly the dreams.

Kate's face, shielded from the searing sun by one of her grandmother's beloved Chicago Cubs baseball caps, remained impassive. Even if her eyes saw the trail, it was memory guiding her. Kate gave her surroundings little notice. Her mind, crammed full of weighty matters, could not be bothered with the scenery along a desolate route she knew so well.

Orville kept ahead a bit; perching patiently on a low jutting, rock outcropping, a wizened tree limb, or a jumble of decaying lumber. He watched protectively over Kate and, with nary a whimper of complaint, cheerfully accepted the physical therapy she had forced upon him. Nay, rather he rejoiced in it—to fly again was glorious!

Near the midway point, Orville perched leisurely on a roughly hewn fencepost leaning next to the trail. Never painted, it had assumed the color of death—shadowy gray.

The fence's horizontal rails had rotted away long ago, giving the solitary post a rather forlorn, deserted appearance.

As Kate approached his resting place, unable to make eye contact because of her downcast concentration, he opened his wings wide, alerting her to his presence so as not to startle and perhaps frighten her.

The movement caught her eye and smiling widely she paused, gathering Orville gently into her arms. "Thank you for waiting, Orvie. It's nice to have a friend along."

As she gently stroked his head with her hand he stretched his neck upward like a petted cat appreciating the touch and seeking more. "If it's okay with you I need to get something off my chest. It's been bothering me for a long time. I haven't told Mom or Gramma about it because they worry about me enough as it is. As for Dad, well, he just wouldn't understand. You know how dads can be."

She shifted Orville into the crook of her arm, balancing him more comfortably and taking his weight on her hip, like a mother with her toddler while chatting with a friend in the mall parking lot.

"There are people at my school," she began, "quite a few actually, who don't like me. Of course, I do have a couple of friends, but they're just like I am, and I want to be friends with everyone—not just the smart kids. These people I'm talking about, the ones who don't like me, think because I love to read and write I'm weird. Not fun weird, if you know what I mean. Bad weird. It's not like I'm a brown nose or anything, but they've hung the label on me, and it really hurts. It's just, I really enjoy school, Orvie; it's fun talking to the teachers, joking around and teasing them.

"As you've no doubt already noticed, I love reading novels and writing poems, not serious poetry or anything, but you know—simple rhymes like the kind Gramma writes. I enjoy learning about history and math, finding out about other places in the world, and sharing what I've learned. But, for some reason, people can't accept I love school. They resent I earn all A's and the teachers like me."

Kate paused in her confession and for a few silent moments tenderly caressed Orville's head and back feathers.

"Last year three girls who I thought were my friends said some awful things about me. They spread poisonous lies and ugly words about me all around the school. They really hurt my feelings, but I didn't tell anyone because I didn't want them to get in trouble, even though they deserved it. It makes me sad to have my classmates think about me in such a mean way. We've all been together and friends since kindergarten, and if they liked me and thought I was fun before, why not now? Have I changed, or have they?"

Orville sensed correctly Kate's questions were merely rhetorical ones, and she didn't really expect him to reply. He was troubled by her obvious melancholy and longed to say something to comfort her. For now, he snuggled tight to her side and remained silent. To red-tailed hawks, a silent listener is the very best kind.

"Most of the kids in our school are as smart as I am and could get good grades if they tried a little harder. Well, school begins again in just a few more days, right after

Labor Day, and I'm worried they will start over with their mean stories about me. Do you know how I feel?" Kate's eyes had pooled up and she lifted her hand and wiped under her nose. "Was school ever terrible for you?"

Orville squirmed and twisted in Kate's arm so he could see her face and make eye contact. His beak opened, and with great effort, two simple intelligible answers to Kate's questions were uttered. "Yes, understand Kate feelings. But, all classmates love Orville. And Orville love all classmates." His eyes sympathetically solemn, blinked twice.

"Orville top student," he continued. "Same Kate. One different. We red-tails—one for all, all for one. Teacher Higgins pound in heads. Everyday Higgins insists everybody love everybody. No possible dislike classmate." He paused a moment, then asked, "What brown nose, Kate? Not understand. Same broccoli and Yankees?"

Kate giggled loudly, stretching her tear-stained cheeks. Orville's reply had gladdened her heart and dried her eyes. She pulled him up to her chest and for a long moment she hugged him tight, her heartbeat echoing his heartbeat. Finally, she released her embrace and gingerly placed him back on the fence post.

Wrinkling her face in distaste she said, "Brown nose is an awful, ugly expression. It's meant to be funny, but is definitely not. It's crude and very hurtful. Broccoli is a vegetable I should eat more of, but the texture and taste are dreadful. Grampa refused to eat it his whole life, and I guess I caught it from him. As you already know, the Yankees are a baseball team in the American league. Don't get me started on the Yankees. All I'll say is they're way rich and buy all the hotshot players so they win the American League pennant practically every year. I much prefer the Chicago Cubs."

Kate had opened her trusting heart to Orville and now, her spirit rebalanced by his empathy, made whatever might happen at school next week or even a month from now, weigh less heavily on her troubled shoulders.

"I'm glad you were a good student too, Orvie. Thanks for listening. I feel way better already. It's nice to have a friend who understands. It reminds me of something I read in a book called *Giants of the Earth* last year: 'Two can carry what one alone cannot lift.' It reminds me of my great-grandparents and all the homesteaders who had to sacrifice and work together to make a successful life here in South Dakota." She patted Orville's head. "C'mon friend, let's go catch some fish."

Within an hour Kate had pulled a small sand shiner to the bank, removed the hook, and fed the flopping fish to Orville, who forgot how unusually tired his wings felt. Someone had piled rocks around a heat-blackened fire pit, and he rested gratefully on a small pile of brushwood nearby.

After an hour more of fruitless casting Kate waded ashore and announced, "They're not biting. Time to eat." Digging through her backpack, she said, "How about some chips and half a tuna sandwich? I hope you like dill pickles and mayo." She sat down on the riverbank next to Orville. Tearing off a bite-sized chunk of white bread, lettuce, and tuna laced with chopped pickle, she presented it to him.

"Trrrr," he said, taking it carefully from her outstretched fingers.

They sat comfortably close, side-by-side, ground dweller and flyer, sharing food, air, water, and affection—the bounty of contentment—life. The chips, sandwiches, apple, and carrot sticks soon disappeared, and Kate rummaged through her bag for the ever-present book. "Are you ready to read?"

For the next thirty minutes Kate flogged their imaginations with images of Bilbo Baggins desperately clinging to a wildly rolling wine barrel being dragged down a treacherous and icy river, not at all like the placid Moreau meandering casually by a few feet in front of them. At chapter's end, with Mr. Baggins safe at last, Kate softly closed the book.

"Time for a swim," she announced, discarding the Cubs baseball cap and kicking off her shoes.

Leaving Orville resting contentedly near the bank, she waded out waist deep, and then, porpoise like, arched her back and dived under like a pliant spear. The river's tepid surface enveloped her and she pulled herself nearer the bottom, seeking cooler water, and then allowed herself to glide silently downstream with the timid current.

Orville's head swiveled, anxiously following her dark shadow, much like a World War II sailor helplessly watching from the deck of a destroyer as a deadly German torpedo plows harmlessly by the bow of his ship. Ten seconds, twenty seconds, thirty seconds of silence elapsed and then her head broke through the surface sixty yards downstream. Immediately, with crisp, slicing strokes and a powerful flutter kick, she swam back upstream against the helpless flow.

Adjacent to Orville's perch she dived under again, emerging a few seconds later in a sudden explosion of shattered surface, spitting air and water. With cupped hands, a teasing Kate splashed water at Orville, who flexed his wings and prudently kept his distance. Cooled and refreshed, she waded ashore, squeezing her dripping braid like a thick-fingered washerwoman working her sheets. Feeling the heat again, she replaced her baseball cap, snugging it down to her eyebrows. She retrieved her pole, re-baited the hook with a wriggling worm and waded knee deep, fishing a dark, shadowy hole partially shaded by a steep bank and a few gangly trees clinging to the opposite side.

When her pole tip dipped, and the line snapped taut, Orville flapped his wings wildly as Kate waded deeper and leaned back, bending the pole almost in half. The surface roiled violently in an unseen fight for life, and Kate walked backward up the bank, dragging a medium size catfish against its will, in the general direction of the Flannery dinner table.

"One more of these and we're in the supper business." She held the wriggling fish up for Orville to see. "Isn't he a beauty?" Her face, flushed from the morning walk, the shared lunch, Bilbo Baggins's thrilling river adventure, her swim, and the brilliant sunshine, radiated pure, youthful happiness. Likewise, Orville; although it's much more difficult to read joy on a hawk's face. For humans, a happy face wrinkles gleefully into a wide smile, while for red-tailed hawks it's all in the eyes—a soft glitter—like emeralds laid gently on yellow silk.

Before they headed home forty-five minutes later, Orville ravenously gulped down a small carp, and Kate wrapped two glistening *ictalurus punctatus* in wet grass and placed them at the bottom of her pack. Quickly she unclipped her reel, stuffed it in the pack's side pocket, and approached Orville with the bare pole in hand.

"Hey Orvie, carry this home for me, will you, please? I need your help again." She extended her tanned arms and held the pole out.

Orville blinked his eyes, once, twice, and launched himself. He hovered momentarily like an overgrown hummingbird in front of Kate and then, grasping the pole in one powerful talon, slowly winged off southward toward the ranch.

"Don't wait for me," she shouted. "I'll be along. Get on home. Do be careful of your leg. Please don't say anything to Gramma about what I told you today. That brown nose stuff is just between us, okay?"

Orville, progressively fatigued from his physical therapy, the reading, and a day under the hot sun, fought to get airborne; the drag created by his leg cast and the fishing pole challenged his strength, but with some difficulty he slowly gained altitude and glanced over his left shoulder at the figure of a waving Kate, gradually diminishing in size below.

Laboriously he turned, banking back toward the river like an outbound airliner asked to return to the runway by air traffic control. He circled Kate once and then, certain his friend no longer needed him, flapped methodically toward the ranch.

Chapter Twelve
A Secret Revealed

The Prairie Winds P.T.A. had spent two feverish hours the prior evening festooning the Hawk's Nest, as the school cafeteria was called, with red and gold balloons and streamers to lend an air of majesty to the annual graduation dinner. Even though the final exams had not yet been graded, it was a foregone conclusion all the fledglings would pass and graduate.

The cafeteria staff had prepared a magnificent meal for the occasion, and beaming parents joined the students at the tables. When Dr. Bennington, Nurse Nan, and Boyd Higgins entered the building most of the parents and students had already filled their trays. The room hummed with happy chatter.

Higgins stood in the doorway for a moment and surveyed the excited throng of young scholars. He had just completed a long and exasperating conference with Dr. Ridgefield, the school district superintendent. Ridgefield had concluded Orville would be allowed to graduate, but his appointment to the academy would be voided due to "visual limitations." He then instructed

Higgins to replace the academy scholarship and Gold Medal awards with the next best student.

With a heavy heart thudding dully in his chest, Higgins scanned the room until he spotted Orville, seated next to his mother, father, and aging grandmother. As the first in his family to graduate from flight school, Orville's achievement, no doubt, was a colossal honor for the Hampstead family.

If only they knew Orville's classmates had already voted him Flyer of the Year; and earlier that morning Higgins had been prepared to honor him with the Gold Medal as class valedictorian. Even more monumental, Orville had been selected by the South Dakota Hawk Squadron as a Commended Flyer and won a coveted scholarship to Higgins's own alma mater, the Flight Academy in Pierre. It was perfectly clear to RT Boyd Higgins that bigger eyes than his own had been watching Orville's talent from afar.

Higgins legs wobbled and he began to sweat profusely. "Go ahead, Dr. Bennington." He pointed to the food line and stack of trays. Higgins tried his best to smile. "I'm really not very hungry, and I need to polish my speech. I'll join you and Nurse Nan for dessert in a few minutes," he mumbled, slowly extricating a folded sheet of paper from his vest pocket.

He beat a hasty retreat to his office and stared forlornly at the words he had written a week ago when it had been perfectly clear Orville was the truly outstanding student of the year. His mind whirled as he tried to imagine whom else to consider? Yes, Amelia was a terrific flyer, along with Orville, probably the best of the bunch. But, he considered Amelia to be a bit of a risk taker and had chosen Orville over her.

Lindy, stronger and almost as acrobatic in the air as Amelia, was also an obvious candidate. Lindy's math scores and SATs were a fraction behind Orville's. Armstrong had finished the year second to Orville academically, but was, at best, an average flyer, never quite mastering the more complicated dive sequences. Horatio, the beloved class clown, could stalk and knock a gnat out of the air in a gale, but was a total twit in the classroom. Higgins sighed. He had little choice but to honor Amelia over Orville.

A sudden loud knock on the office door interrupted his frantic calculations. "Yes?" he called out. "It's open. Come in, please."

The door creaked open. There stood Annabelle and Sally, smiling nervously. Sally said, "Mr. Higgins, sir, the cake and ice cream are being served. One of the P.T.A. ladies asked us to find you and remind you of the award ceremony immediately following dessert."

"Thank you," he replied, mustering the best smile he could under the dismal circumstances. "I'll be there in just a minute." Trying his best to sound cheerful, he said, "Please save me a big slab of cake and ice cream," though in fact his stomach was churning with indecision and eating was distant to his mind.

Moments later Higgins was seated next to Nurse Nan, toying with his spoon around a mountain of melting, vanilla ice cream. The trays, for the most part, had been deposited in the scullery and the room gradually quieted down into hushed anticipation. Someone dimmed the overhead lights and a spotlight focused on the small, elevated stage used for drama and award presentations.

Horatio's mother, the P.T.A. chairhawk, fluttered up to the stage. She was somewhat chunky and wore a bit too much make-up, but she was appreciated for the endless hours she and the other mothers had volunteered for the school's benefit. She opened her wings wide, tapped nervously on the microphone, and said, "Testing, one, two, three."

Horatio, seated nearby, stood and shouted, "Howdy doody, Mom!" Higgins lowered his eyes and cringed at Horatio's talent for directing attention to himself.

Ignoring her outspoken son, she addressed the audience. "The Prairie Winds P.T.A. members welcome you to this year's class graduation. It has been a terrific year for us. Speaking for the P.T.A. and all the parents, I would like to express our sincere appreciation to Mr. Higgins, and also to the entire Prairie Winds staff for their outstanding efforts to educate our fledglings."

She stepped back from the microphone as applause rained down. It was Horatio who started the chant: "Higgins, Higgins, Higgins."

Finally Higgins stood, somehow forced a smile, and waved a wing at the crowd.

What he really wanted to do was fly right out the door and never come back. What he had to do next would be the most difficult task of his teaching career.

Finally the chant subsided and the chairhawk stepped back to the microphone. Beaming broadly, she said, "In a few minutes Mr. Higgins will present the Flyer of the Year selection and award the Gold Medal to the class valedictorian. Before I turn over the microphone I must give a huge thank you to my co-chair, Marge Harris, and the entire decorating committee for magically transforming this rather drab cafeteria into such a colorful graduation palace."

She gestured toward the audience and directed, "Marge, could you and your helpers stand, please?"

For once Higgins was grateful the speaker was carrying on. He closed his eyes and tried to concentrate while applause for the decorators, office staff, food service workers, secretaries, and finally, Tom Cooper the school custodian, filled the room.

Nurse Nan nudged Higgins. "Mr. Higgins," she whispered, "you're on."

Trembling, he stood, sipped his water, wiped his beak with a napkin, and slowly climbed the four steps to the stage. As he looked out over the crowd, just as he had for the past twelve years, an incredible calmness engulfed him. He loved these hawks. They trusted him with their most precious possessions—their fledglings—and his students trusted him with their most precious dreams—their futures.

Higgins knew whatever he was forced to say, the Prairie Winds community would accept his words no matter how disappointing they might be for Orville and his family. Besides, under any other circumstances, Amelia was a truly outstanding flyer and well worthy of the Gold Medal honor.

Higgins took a deep breath, steadied himself, and began. "Each year the members of the graduating class vote for a classmate whom they believe to be the best example of what a red-tailed hawk flyer should be. To make their selection, the students consider courage, maneuverability, navigation skill, stamina, integrity, and kindness." Higgins paused, trying to swallow the growing lump in his throat.

"These are the qualities all of us red-tails cherish. We faculty members are not allowed to vote on the nominees, nor are we permitted to change the outcome of the vote. I personally counted the votes along with the student body president, Andrew Martinez, and our vice president, Sophie Davis. We three are the only ones who, at this moment, know the name of this year's honoree. I invite Andy and Sophie to the stage."

The room erupted with applause as the two most popular students made their way to the platform. When it was quiet again, Higgins said, "Andy, please announce the name of this year's Flyer of the Year award."

Andy leaned toward the microphone, blushed, and faced the crowd. Grinning widely he blurted, "Orville, buddy, you're the best. Dude, come on up!"

The crowd stood and thunderous applause escorted Orville up the steps. Clearly pleased, he hugged Sophie and high-fived Andy.

Higgins's eyes had filled with tears. He carefully opened a small box and walked to the edge of the platform. Then he held up, for all to see, the shimmering silver chain, which was threaded through a pair of magnificent silver wings. He handed the chain to Sophie, and as she placed it around Orville's neck, Horatio started the chant: "Orville, Orville, Orville."

No one had ever seen Orville flustered or at a loss for words before, but now his face was almost as red as his tail feathers as he stood mute before the microphone.

Finally, Higgins walked forward, leaned, and said, "Perhaps you'd care to say something, Flyer of the Year." While the audience laughed, Higgins stepped back, folded his wings, and took a deep breath. *Thankfully*, he thought, *it'll all be over in a few minutes*.

Orville beamed at the audience. "First off, I want to thank my classmates for encouraging me and putting up with me this year. I truly wish there were thirty Flyer of the Year awards, as each of my classmates deserves one. On the first day of school last September, Mr. Higgins challenged us to become the best flyers in all of South Dakota. I don't know if we have earned such an awesome distinction or not, but I do know all thirty of us gave it our best shot, and to our teacher, RT Boyd Higgins, we will be eternally grateful." Applause engulfed the room.

"I also would like to thank my family and other school staff for their constant loving support and encouragement. Truly, I owe a huge debt of gratitude to Mr. Cooper, our custodian, who helped me open my locker on all those days when I couldn't remember my combo." Another roar of approval erupted from the crowd.

Then, unexpectedly, Orville stepped back and removed the silver chain from about his neck. "Grandmother, Mom, and Dad, could you come up here for a moment, please?" The crowd fell silent as an elderly, gray-feathered hawk, holding tightly to Orville's parents slowly climbed to the stage. Once there they hugged Orville and stood to one side.

The silence and early evening shadows further darkened the room, transforming Orville's figure into a sharp silhouette. His voice was a soft whisper as he began. "I have a secret to reveal."

He turned and faced his parents. "Mom, Dad, I'm sorry Grandmother and I didn't share this with you earlier. This is a family secret, Grandmother whispered in my ear one night last winter while she was in the hospital critical care unit with pneumonia and not expected to live more than a few hours."

Orville glanced over at his grandmother. She stared out at the hushed audience before her, wings demurely folded. Orville opened his right wing and tenderly wrapped it lovingly around her shoulders.

"Grandmother was afraid something she had done as a fledgling would taint our family forever, but in reality, it has made us better hawks, and I love her all the more for it." Orville's eyes glistened in the shadows and his voice caught momentarily in his throat. "You see," he finally said, "when Grandmother was very young she fell head over talons in love with an owl."

There was an audible gasp from below. Someone said, loud enough for all to hear, "I don't believe it. No red-tail could ever love an owl."

Another voice from the back squawked, "Shame on her."

Ignoring the hurtful comments and the crowd's murmurs, Orville continued, "A few weeks after the wedding up in Minnesota, Grandmother's new husband, my grandfather, Ollie, whom I never got to meet, was shot and killed for sport by a mindless timber worker. Utterly grief-stricken, she flew alone back home here to South Dakota. Then she hatched and raised my mom all by herself. As you're all aware, Grandmother never remarried."

Orville paused, and the audience, seemingly mesmerized and collectively holding its breath, waited for his next words.

"My mother, without realizing it until this very moment, is one-half owl. And I am one-fourth owl. Neither my mother nor I can see clearly in bright light. Mom has had to wear sunglasses every day since she was a fledgling to protect her eyes." He smiled at his mom and said, "Dad and I always tease her about wanting to be a movie star. She's certainly got those Bette Davis eyes, don't you think?"

Mrs. Hampstead reached up with a steady wingtip and pulled her sunglasses off. She smiled and waved them high over her head.

When the laughter died down, Orville said, "Mom and I can still fly, and even hunt, but we lose clarity and depth perception whenever the daytime sky is brightly lit." Orville stepped to the side and hugged his mom. "But," he said, returning to the microphone, "you ought to see us after dark. We can flat out cruise!"

The cafeteria reverberated with more laughter.

"Grandmother wanted me to know her secret so I would understand why if I flunked out of flight school." He grinned widely and said, "I guess you didn't have to worry after all, Gram."

The audience exploded with shouts of approval as Orville placed the Wings of Flight around his grandmother's neck and then, in the ultimate demonstration of a hawk's affection, rubbed the side of his beak against his grandmother's.

A few minutes later with his eyes still wet, Higgins, with a sudden change of heart, awarded the Gold Medal for academic excellence to Lindy and announced Amelia had been selected as the school's first ever Commended Flyer and would be attending the prestigious Flight Academy on scholarship. Orville, his family, and everyone else in the audience stood and cheered her selection. What Higgins had to say doesn't really matter. What Orville had already said was enough.

And so it came to pass, RT Orville Hampstead, on a beautiful August day, dove fearlessly through Beth Flannery's dazzling wash to attack her husband's work boot, caught a wingtip on an invisible strand of braided steel clothesline wire, and darn near brained himself. Extenuating circumstances, indeed!

Chapter Thirteen

Water, Water, Everywhere

AWKS, FORGED BY NATURE'S SMITHY, SOFTENED by flame and hammered to shape on the anvil of life, experience incredible daily hardships. Likewise, South Dakota's history documents bone-chilling accounts of the early immigrants' travels west across America. America's fresh newcomers traveled day after day through hostile, unknown territory at a slug's pace, not knowing what lay ahead or even sure where their final destination would be.

Not everyone, it seems, had their eyes fixed on California gold or the opportunities presented in the vast pristine wilderness of the Oregon Territory. Along the way, for whatever reasons, the head of a family, his wife and children riding stoically alongside, might slowly pull their wagon out of the line and let the others pass. Shading his eyes against the blinding western sun, a weary husband might mutter through cracked lips, "Far enough for us, sweet lady wife."

Or a single man, rifle butt resting on shoulder, trudging along in the choking dust beside a matched pair of oxen, might turn aside, watch the others roll on, and bravely declare, "Far enough. Not going another step. This here dirt is as good as any."

Sometimes "far enough" was in land known then as the Dakotas. The first need—as the relative safety and comfort provided by the company of their fellow travelers vanished into the horizon—no matter how tired, ill, or hungry these drop-offs might be, was water.

Björn Dahl, twenty-two years old, less than a year removed from his Norwegian homeland, had been one of these. One pocket contained less than twenty dollars; the other, less than twenty words of English. He had chosen a most difficult path and stopped near a place destined to become, many years later, Dupree, South Dakota.

With the late afternoon sun moving off to her right, Kate walked briskly toward the Flannery ranch house. Orville, his cast leg dragging, winged slowly off in a nearly straight line, heading due south of the riverbank. Kate's route, however, followed a meandering course of least resistance in the general direction of her home. Originally it had been no more than a scant deer trail leading down to the river. No doubt early members of the Cheyenne River Sioux who populated the nearby land also treaded the nearly indiscernible route from time to time.

Eventually homesteaders like Björn Dahl arrived. They too used the path and perhaps even tried to mark or improve it. But now, time, wind, and periodic rinses from the sky at unpredictable times of the year swept clean almost all traces of foot traffic from the seldom-used trail.

Kate kept her head down, both as protection from the blazing sun's glare as it slid relentlessly toward the western seas and the distant lands beyond—and to make certain she traveled true.

There was a low rising butte just ahead, serving as a signpost for the few who ventured there. The path then turned sharply to the east to skirt the butte. Kate knew instinctively the shorter, straighter route would be directly over the butte and down the other side where she could easily pick up the path again. However, the strict dictum to never stray off the established way had been drummed into her and came as the price of her freedom to go fishing alone.

Grampa Ernie had often cautioned young Kate about the necessity of sticking to the path, and about the risk of getting lost and wandering for days before being found. In the same vein, her father sometimes read tragic newspaper articles to her about hunters and fishermen who became disoriented by the endless, unmarked prairie and consequently died of thirst or cold.

Disregarding her elders' wisdom, a hungry and tired Kate detoured off the pathway and turned directly south toward the butte. Youthful disregard of parental instruction is nothing new, but sometimes results in dire consequences.

When she reached the crest of the steep-faced promontory she was breathing hard; she slid her backpack off to sit down and rest for a moment on a nearby boulder. Elevated fifty yards or so, her vista was panoramic and she caught sight of, far off in the distance, a cloud of dust rising from the Iron Mountain road leading south to Red Elm and Dupree.

"Wonder who that could be?" she muttered. "Too late for the mailman, and Gramma doesn't drive anymore. Mom and Dad are probably halfway to Rapid City by now." She squinted into the sun, but other than the billowing rooster-tail of dust from the road, could make out nothing specific.

After a brief rest she stood and turned around to see back the way she had come. The river, perhaps a mile away, was now just a blue ribbon slicing through the desolate prairie. Kate took a long drink from her plastic water bottle, licked her parched lips, tipped her head back, and drained it.

"Best get going so Gramma doesn't worry," she said, her voice small and unheard. She recapped the empty bottle and dropped it into her pack.

The tabletop of land was a few hundred yards wide and soon enough Kate marched stiff legged down the rocky slope of the far side toward flat ground. As she gingerly picked her way down the slope, she noticed, just off to her right, a cluttered mound where long ago a hardy Norwegian homesteader had first built a crude, dirt-floor sod shack. The settler survived the first few years and his feet were solidly planted on the land. A permanent frame house was eventually built, along with a nearby barn for the animals. Thus the original sod house, no longer needed as a residence, became useful as an auxiliary tool and seed storage shed.

However, all of these original structures had now succumbed to the relentless effects of time and weather, and lay in a jumbled heap. A few gray support timbers remained along with a small pile of broken chimney bricks scattered helter-skelter and darkened by time. Much more recently someone had broken a beer bottle and the amber shards caught the sun's rays and hurled them back into deep space. Determined deep-rooted prairie grass surrounded and infiltrated the burial heap, creating an indistinct layering of the landscape.

Curious, Kate veered several yards west toward the reclaimed fragment. Vaguely she wondered about the family who had lived there. Her grandfather had told her many stories of the early Scandinavian and Irish immigrants, and just a year earlier she had read her grandmother's copy of *Giants in the Earth,* a heartbreaking novel by O.E. Rölvaag of a Norwegian family's attempt to make a home in the hostile Dakotas.

Kate was aware the locals referred to this section of the river where it snaked into a broad turn as Dahl's Bend. She sometimes wondered if Dahl had been a lonely and desperate outlaw with hideous beard and long, filthy hair hiding from the authorities, running from the long arm of New York law. Or had he just been another adventurous, handsome young man, who somehow could convince a beautiful, soft-handed Norwegian lady to sail the stormy Atlantic with him and ride a wagon across the vast prairie to the Dakotas to begin a new and better life. No one, her grandfather included, seemed to know for sure.

Bundled against the cold, did Dahl and his wife cuddle together under a heavy pile of blankets, gleaning hope from the Bible by candlelight, in a futile search for the strength to survive yet another nightmarish epoch of interminable South Dakota winter? Grampa Ernie Flannery had reveled in spinning stories of the old-timers who according to him were like wind-blown chunks of Velcro, flying through the air and sticking to the land here and there. A few of these tales might even have been true.

Kate smiled at the thought of her grandfather's angelic face shining innocently at the dinner table, his blue eyes sparkling with pleasure, in the middle of an outrageous exaggeration or even, if need be, an out and out lie about his own boyhood or the founders of the prairie. She wondered if, when she became old and gray, she would have adventurous stories to tell of her own life, or would she be forced to merely repeat and embellish the ones her grandfather had shared so many happy evenings around the Flannery dinner table. Kate's present life seemed so ordinary and unremarkable, she couldn't imagine what interesting tales she might spin to her own grandchild in the distant future.

Kate carefully picked her way through the jumble of antique timbers and bricks. Seeing nothing of interest, she turned and headed once again in the direction she knew would soon intersect with the path leading back to the ranch.

About fifty yards from the crumbled house she caught her toe, stumbled awkwardly, then stepped hard onto a gone pulpy plank. As it gave way beneath her she let out a sharp yelp, like a pup whose tail has been accidentally closed in the screen door. Instinctively Kate threw out her hands and tried to grab something, anything, but all was decayed, nothing firm.

She fell silently as hunting hawks fall to gain maximum acceleration and surprise. A third of the way down, the toe of her tennis shoe caught on one side of the vertical shaft; the impact was as sharp and quick as a hangman's noose around a condemned man's neck. Her knee held for a fraction of an instant until her chin slammed into it, stunning her; then she was thrown viciously against the opposite wall. Loose dirt and pebbles cascaded down with her as she hit the water on her back with a tremendous splash.

Momentarily unconscious, Kate floated for two or three seconds until her head dipped under. A mouthful of fetid water brought her back, and her piercing scream spiraled up the rocky sides, spilling out the small entrance she had just created in the well's ancient cover.

Then there was dreadful silence and except for the eye of a tiny torn window, forty-five feet above, total darkness. The water, blacker than moonless midnight, lapped like a probing serpent's tongue at the well's sides and licked hungrily at Kate's slender neck. Too terror-stricken to investigate below with her feet, she desperately treaded the murky water with adrenaline-powered arms.

Exactly six hundred and fifty feet above the opening of Björn Dahl's long forgotten well, Orville's former classmate, Annabelle, returning swiftly home from a successful day of hunting, slowed. She alone had heard Kate's blood-curdling shriek.

Annabelle banked sharply toward the stabbing cry and screeched at the golden sun: "Klisssss!"

The feathered huntress took particular note of the spot where a small, royal blue baseball cap lay.

Conscientiously, she studied the distinctive capital letter C in bright red, outlined in white, emblazoned on the cap. Checking her wing watch and then, sighting carefully over one extended wing, noted the height of the setting sun on the horizon; she fixed the location in her mind—though for what possible reason she knew not. The baseball cap rode the prairie like a bright beacon of hope, floating to mark the spot where a foundered ship and its luckless crew had been swallowed by the trembling sea. Puzzled how a Chicago Cubs baseball cap and a scream of terror could possibly exist in such a lonely place, Annabelle circled once more.

Abruptly, she wheeled north and hurried on.

Chapter Fourteen

Nor Rhyme nor Reason

WITHIN MINUTES OF LEAVING KATE ON THE bank of the river, Orville arrived back home. He descended wearily and carefully deposited Kate's fishing rod on the clotheslines where he had picked it up earlier in the day. Unusually fatigued from carrying the extra burden, and not knowing what else to do but wait, he settled heavily on his radio perch under the sheltering apple tree.

Shortly, he heard the screen door on the back porch squeak open and then bang shut; a minute later, Gramma, garden scissors in hand, bustled around the corner. Intent on cutting a clutch of fresh flowers from the garden to complement her dinner table setting, she didn't at first notice Orville.

Swiveling his head, owl-like, he observed silently as she wandered, back bent, from dahlia to dahlia snipping colorful dessert-plate-sized blooms here and there. Satisfied she had gathered enough for her vase, she straightened her back and turned toward the apple tree.

Catching sight of the motionless hawk, and somewhat startled, she said, "Oh, hi, Orville. If you will, tell why you perch so still." Without waiting for a reply, she added, "Is our Kate back yet? The table's all set."

She walked over to Orville and held the bouquet up to his beak. "Don't these have a wonderful fragrance? Makes my nostrils prance and dance."

Orville, exercising poetic restraint, merely grinned. *She has no idea how powerful a hawk's senses are,* he thought. *I caught the flowers' scent each time she cut a stem.*

Gramma continued with an optimistic rhyme, "Our Kate will be along soon. I shan't sing a worried tune." She reached out and gently stroked Orville's feathered head. "I do hope she caught some fish. If not, hotdogs and beans will fill our dish."

Glancing down at the gold watch her husband had given her on their fiftieth wedding anniversary, just three years earlier, she said, "It's coming up on five. Surely she'll soon arrive." The corner of the house blocked her view of the driveway leading up to the house, but she glanced nervously there anyway. "I see you've returned the fishin' pole. Your commendable work, I extol."

Feeling the slight chill of the night's early shadows, Gramma had draped a light sweater over her bony shoulders. Glancing over at Orville, she shivered. "Won't be long till autumn is here. Another cold season, I fear." She turned toward the house. "Please wait here while I dunk these flowers in water. Be a good hawk, sir. Keep the watch. Don't dare stir."

For the next thirty minutes, Gramma paced a nervous sentinel's post at the big window in front of the kitchen sink. Her eyes continuously surveyed the general direction Kate would be returning, and as each minute passed, her concern and anxiety mounted. At half past five she pulled her thin arms into the sweater's sleeves and hurried out the back door. Approaching Orville, like a lonesome person might talk to a pet dog, cat, or even an indoor plant, she asked the pertinent question, "I'm getting worried. Surely Kate hurried?"

Gramma's apprehensive tone caused Orville to spread his wings wide and then refold them. The growing tension fueled by her worry jumbled the poetry as she rambled. "Was she okay when you left her, Orville? I don't think I can walk so far anymore. Maybe I can. It's been years since I've been out to the river. Kate took swimming lessons down at Dupree every summer. People say she's a real good swimmer. Oh, Kate, dear Kate, where are you?"

Gramma shivered again and crossing her arms across her chest, hugged herself. "Do you think I should call Dave and Beth? I don't want to worry them for nothing, and it would take at least four hours to drive back here from Rapid City. They could be eating dinner in a restaurant. Will their cell phone ring there? Or do people turn them off while they eat? Surely Kate'll be along soon."

She rubbed her bony fingers nervously along her thighs. "If I can locate the truck keys, maybe I could drive out there and pick her up. Dave says the truck drives real easy. I haven't had a license for fifteen years, but I'm sure I can still drive. The police won't care since this is an emergency. What do you think we should do, Orville?"

On the verge of tears, she continued, "Kate didn't fall in the river, did she? It wouldn't be very deep this late in the summer, would it? Maybe she's just twisted her ankle on a slippery rock and can't walk."

Fraught with desperation, thin lips barely moving, she prayed, "Loving God, wrap your strong arms around our Kate, hold her up, and keep her safe." And, "Orville, won't you please, please do something?"

As if given permission to exercise his own growing concern for Kate's whereabouts, and responding to Gramma's anxious request, Orville immediately elevated, spread his wings, fanned his tail feathers, maneuvered awkwardly around the house corner and vanished.

Gramma, her lips barely moving, whispered in her old-fashioned manner, "God be with ye, hawk." With those ancient words of faith still lingering in the air, she hurried around the corner. Orville was already out of sight. She scampered up the steps and into the house.

"It's so cold," she said. Her hand shook uncontrollably on the knob as she pushed the door open.

Orville's talons grabbed mud in a perfect, one-legged touch down at river's edge where he had taken the pole from Kate. It was brutally quiet now. The grass growing along the bank undulated in obedient waves as the early evening wind followed the river's curves and indentations. The water rippled as well, but more conspicuously it was a splendid mirror of shimmering diamonds, reflecting the hurrying sun's farewell rays.

For birds dwelling in metropolises like Los Angeles, Madrid, and Berlin, the constant and overpowering city noise extinguishes the distinctness of sounds, merging each separate sound into an insistent roar; on the other hand, South Dakota hawks, trained in surveillance techniques and raised in the utter silence of bare land, are crisply tuned in to all the frequencies of nature.

To Orville's ear the gurgle of the flowing river against protruding rocks was clearly separate from the skimming of the wind over the water's surface. So too, was the faint scraping sounds made by countless strands of pliant prairie grass rubbing their shoulders together. Orville strained to hear sounds clashing with nature. But to his ear, the orchestra of the wilderness crooned in harmony, just as directed from the podium of the South Dakota plains. He neither heard nor saw anything unusual.

In his hasty quest to find Kate, Orville had navigated a low level flight exactly above the path she had traversed earlier in the day—from the ranch house, to the spot he had last gazed upon her as she waved goodbye to him. Then he realized the error of his logic: *If Kate had simply retraced the original path she almost certainly would have arrived back home long ago. She must have chosen a different route.*

Orville refused to allow himself to consider other nagging possibilities: Kate was in the river. Or, someone or something had snatched her up. These thoughts his mind forbade.

Chapter Fifteen
The Dreadful Truth

KATE WAS NUMB. HER HEART HAD AT FIRST BEAT furiously with the unutterable fear of drowning, but within minutes of her fall her mind had discovered a dull, insulated island of safety. Her initial panic gradually subsided, and now she allowed her legs to sag and investigate the depths below her. She was astonished to realize the toes on her left foot touched bottom.

Taking stock, she noticed a terrible throbbing in her right leg, and putting any weight on it exacted excruciating pain. She could taste warm blood in her mouth where her teeth had sliced her tongue and lips when her chin struck her knee. She spat and said, "Yuck!"

Standing on a left-footed tiptoe, the water barely covered her shoulders and lapped lightly at her throat. Kate's braid had partially unraveled at impact and now floated like a frayed rope behind her.

Thinking more clearly with each passing moment, Kate shrugged one arm out of her backpack and let the bag float beside her. Inside the saturated pack, bobbed a one-pound, mostly empty, Folgers coffee can with a blue plastic lid where she stored her bait worms. She quickly realized the buoyant can trapped enough air to keep the canvas pack afloat. In her mind, she visualized the interior of the pack and took inventory.

There were two empty plastic water bottles, her soon-to-be water-logged copy of *The Hobbit*, a small pen-shaped emergency flashlight, her fishing reel, a standard-sized glass jar of salmon eggs, and a Zip-lock bag containing extra hooks, leaders, and weights. Two medium-sized channel cats, their destiny of becoming flour and egg-dipped, pan-fried dinner fare interrupted, drifted aimlessly, belly up, next to the coffee can and the bobbing water bottles.

As Kate's breathing and heartbeat slowed, she began to think more rationally. Standing on tiptoe, her head was clearly out of the water; and even flat-footed, her chin was two or three inches above the surface.

Her right tennis shoe had been ripped off her foot when she collided with the wall of the well on her fall through the opening, but otherwise her clothing was intact. Her pack had cushioned her crash landing somewhat, and as she inventoried herself, she realized that, except for a terrible throbbing sensation in her leg and the unpleasant taste of blood in her mouth, she had not been seriously hurt.

Kate zipped open a small, side pocket of the pack and located the tiny flashlight. For the second time since her initial scream of terror, she engaged her voice. Trying hard to remember the last time she had installed fresh batteries, she muttered, "I hope this thing still works."

Holding the flashlight in her right hand, she twisted

the upper segment of it with the fingers of her left, and was rewarded with a bright, narrow beam of light. "Best not waste the batteries," she said, echoing her parents' concern over the need to always conserve energy "just in case" as they put it. She allowed herself a quick smile at the memory of her mother's frequent scoldings for reading late into the night with a flashlight propped on pillows under the bed covers.

Holding the light at arm's length, she played the beam slowly up the cylindrical wall. She hoped to discover a crude rope ladder hanging down the wall like those draped over the sides of wave-tossed pirate ships she had read about; or, at the least, chiseled steps in the steep walls where she might gain a hand hold and somehow drag herself up to the surface, but the walls were completely bare except for gloomy, dark water stains here and there where continuous seeping occurred like unclotted blood oozing from a fresh wound.

Kate had once read a story about "water witching" and when she inquired about it to her Grampa Ernie, he cut a slender, forked branch from a youthful willow tree. With one of the forked ends in each hand, he walked about the yard holding it firmly at arms' length in front of him. Without warning the tip dipped severely, seemingly overpowering Grampa's firm grip, and he let out a holler.

"Dig right here, Kate! There's water down below. The willow can feel it."

His vivid demonstration of "water witching" fired Kate's curiosity. "Do you really believe it works, Grampa?" she had asked.

"Well, I seen it done three or four times over the years, and they always found water, so I'm inclined to think there's something to it. On the other hand, maybe if someone digs deep enough he'll find water any old place."

When Gramma interjected she didn't believe in water witching, he asked her, "Do you believe in Santa Claus?"

"Most certainly," she replied. "Doesn't everybody?"

"What about the tooth fairy?"

Gramma chuckled. "Yes, of course. When I was a kid he stashed a shiny nickel under my pillow for each tooth I lost."

"Here's a tougher question," Grampa said. "Do you believe Noah and his boys built a boat big enough for a male and female of every animal in the world to fit on board and then the whole earth flooded?"

"I used to believe it when I was young," she replied. Her serene face turned wistful.

"But I'm not so sure anymore. Maybe it was just some of the local animals."

"Well, my darling wife, that's pretty much how I feel about water witching." He grinned as wide as a Wyoming box canyon. "Maybe, maybe not. Some things are mighty hard to scientifically verify."

Grampa then explained to Kate about water tables and how vast underground streams flowed deep underneath the earth's surface. He also told her how the early pioneers had a desperate need to locate one of those streams with deep, hand-dug wells.

Then Kate had asked him how they raised the water up to the surface once they found it. At the kitchen table

Grampa had taken a pencil and sketched out a rudimentary design for an elevated winch, allowing for a bucket attached to a rope threaded through a pulley to be lowered, filled with water, and raised to the surface.

He had explained one of his boyhood chores was to carry heavy buckets of water from the well into the house each morning before he went off to school, and how his mother would scold him if he slopped water on her clean, wooden kitchen floor. How Kate wished for such a pulley and rope contraption and her Grampa's strong arms to winch her out and carry her home now!

Kate shone the light directly above her. From her vantage she could see someone had shaped four rough-hewn planks, fastened them together, and covered the well. When she had tripped and accidentally stepped near the center, the rotten planks had crumbled beneath her like the trap door of an executioner's gallows. A fading sliver of dim daylight tentatively poked through the slender opening.

Kate slowly illuminated the wall back again from top to bottom. Then, for a long moment she held the light up high over her head and pointed the beam downward into the water. The thin rays penetrated the surface perhaps an inch or two, but served to calm Kate's nagging fear of sharks, slimy eels, yellow-fanged rats, or other imagined horrors swimming beside her.

She snapped the flashlight off and was plunged again into complete darkness. She knew her eyes were wide open, yet it was as if she were sitting in a dark closet with them tightly closed. An overwhelming urge to cry surged over her and for a few moments she closed her eyes and sobbed. Gradually her anguish ended, and she regained her plucky composure.

"Crying does no good whatsoever, Kate Flannery," she announced loudly. It was a brave statement, but merely an echo of her father's words whenever she resorted to tears at home. Even so, she had desperately needed the tears just now as a bulwark against terror itself.

Thinking more sensibly, she unzipped the bag and snaked her hand inside to remove the worm can. She snapped the plastic lid off, emptied out a bit of dirt and the remaining worms into the water, and placed the flashlight safely inside before replacing the lid. In a far, dry corner of her mind she sensed the flashlight might somehow play a key role in her rescue and must be carefully safeguarded—kept in working order.

In the process of stowing the flashlight away, her hand brushed her soaked book, *The Hobbit,* and she instinctively knew it was already ruined, serving as dead weight inside her pack. Her love for the novel was overruled by her common sense. She pulled the book out and dropped it gently into the murk.

Despite her fervent zeal at home for recycling every scrap of household and yard waste, and her notoriously unpopular stance with many of her classmates on anti-littering at school, she quickly jettisoned the small jar of orange-colored salmon eggs. After a moment of regret, she dropped with a small splash her favorite reel, one her grandfather had used for twenty years, along with the now useless packets of hooks, leaders, and weights.

Likewise she released the two dead catfish into their permanent watery graves. Confident she had done all she could to improve her present situation, she zipped the backpack.

Gazing upward at the tiny shaft of dying light forty-five feet above her, Kate shivered uncontrollably. In a hopeless attempt to keep warm she crossed her arms across her slender chest, placing her hands on opposite shoulders. She scrunched her chin down into the V formed by her crossed arms, hugging herself in a futile attempt to conserve fast dwindling body heat.

"It's so cold," she said, her lips already tinged with ribbons of light blue. "Please hurry, Dad. Please, please, please."

Just then the dreadful truth flooded Kate's mind—her parents were gone for the weekend to Rapid City.

Chapter Sixteen
Self-Reliance

WHEN ORVILLE REALIZED HIS NAVIGATION MIStake, he reasoned Kate must have chosen an alternative route to follow home.

He was very familiar with this territory, hunting in the vicinity of the river frequently. He recalled from one of his "Terrain and Tactics" classes that humans, unlike hawks, are often concerned with choosing the path of least resistance to their destination. He knew the main obstacle between the river and the Flannery ranch was a low butte the trail skirted to the east. Could there be a shorter route avoiding the butte to the west? It was an intriguing possibility. It seemed logical Kate would not have chosen a route of more resistance, uphill over the butte, so he disregarded it as her trekking path.

Heading slightly west and flying low, he scanned every inch of ground between the river and the butte. By this time dusk had defeated daylight; his vision became crystal clear and even small objects appearing fuzzy to him earlier in the day gradually became distinct in the gloaming light. Impatient, he longed for the perfect darkness he knew would bring optimum vision.

There was not a discernible trail, which Orville considered inconsequential, as he knew nature sweeps the prairie each day with gusts of wind and sometimes follows with a brief, rinsing rain. He paused to rest on the western edge of the butte, but seeing and hearing nothing unusual, he gathered his rapidly dwindling strength and continued in an arrow-straight pattern back to the ranch house. He hoped by now Kate had wandered safely home from some secret trail.

The lights were on in the kitchen as Orville approached, and the big window framed Gramma's shape in a dark silhouette. He landed softly on the railing of the back porch, certain she had seen him return.

The back door opened quickly. Gramma emerged wearing a warm jacket and a faded Chicago Cubs baseball cap. "No sign of her yet, Orville?" she questioned. "Where oh where could she be?"

She reached into her pocket and pulled out a set of keys. "We can't just sit and wait any longer. I'm going to drive the truck down to the river. She must have fallen and hurt herself. She's got to be waiting for us out there somewhere. It's going to be completely dark in another fifteen minutes, and we need to find her before then. Let's go, Orv."

Resolute, Gramma walked toward Dave's work truck. "I hope I can figure out how to start this rig," she muttered.

She opened the big door and with both hands reached up and grabbed a pull handle conveniently placed on the inside. She put her left foot on the chrome running board and with a mighty effort pulled herself up. Balanced precariously, she grabbed the steering wheel with her left hand and hoisted herself awkwardly onto the bench seat. Immediately her son's presence invaded her senses, surrounded her, steadied her. The pleasant aroma of his leather boots, his denim jacket, and his sweat lingered, filling the truck cab with an ethereal Dave Flannery, her son, the hard working rancher.

Strengthened and comforted by her son's presence, Gramma bent over and fumbled blindly to find the release handle to move the seat forward. When she located and pulled the mechanism with the fingers on her left hand, she yanked the steering wheel hard with her right and with a quick thrust of her hips the seat obediently slid forward several notches.

"Much better," she said. "I can at least reach the pedals now." She tilted her head to the right and located the ignition slot. Carefully she selected the proper key and inserted it. The arrow on the shifting column was locked in park, just as Dave had left it earlier in the day. Confident now, she turned the key and the big Ford engine roared smoothly to life.

Gramma quickly discovered the switch for the headlights and turned them on. The shifting column now glowed with light, and she pulled the shifting lever down to drive.

"Lucky this is an automatic," she said. "I don't think I could handle a stick shift anymore." Gritting her teeth, she squeezed hard with the thumb on her right hand, managing to release the hand brake and freeing the big truck to lurch forward. There was a large gravel circular turn-around to navigate, and craning her neck forward to see over the hood she somehow managed to steer clear of Beth's decorative bordering flowerbeds.

As the truck slowly headed out the driveway, Orville descended into the back of the pick-up, collapsing gratefully onto a sixty-pound bag of cement.

In 1948, three years after the war ended, a newlywed Susan Flannery, twenty-two years old and a freshly minted University of Illinois graduate with a bachelor's in English, followed her young South Dakota husband, Ernie Flannery, to the desolate land she would call home for the next fifty-six years.

It hadn't been easy for her to make the transition from big city, Chicago career girl to Ziebach County rancher's wife, but love, coupled with time, has a way of smoothing out differences between people, like sharp-edged rocks become polished and smooth in a fast-moving river. Within five years, her longing for the city lights had evaporated like the early morning dew clinging to the prairie grass.

Susan Flannery learned to cook to please her husband and their son, Dave. And when the three of them rode horses to the river for a day of fishing, they carried a sumptuous picnic lunch, and also several sheets of notebook paper. While father and son chased after the elusive fish of the Moreau, and played together in the river, she tucked her skirt around her legs to ward off the flies, sat on the bank, and wrote simple rhymes about her life, her son, her husband, and all things South Dakota wild.

Even though Gramma hadn't been out to the river in several years, she remembered well the three miles of wandering pathway. Darkness had fallen now and she paused momentarily at the intersection of their driveway and the main road near the mailbox. She glanced quickly to the right, straining her eyes down the stretch of twenty-five dusty miles or so where she knew she could find help in Dupree or Red Elm, but out of her anxiety to find Kate, and with the experience of fifty-six years of solving South Dakota problems, often by herself, she hurriedly crossed the road and drove straight toward the river.

It was a bumpy ride, especially for Orville in the back, but the big truck handled the off-road terrain well enough, exactly what it had been designed for. Gramma drove deliberately, bony hands gripping the wheel, her slender shoulders hunched forward over the steering wheel, elbows flexed to the sides like a hawk's folded wings. Her eyes constantly swept from side to side within the range of illumination allowed by the truck's headlights, hoping at any instant to spot an injured Kate sitting by the path with a twisted ankle, waving up at her with the wide familiar grin on her young face.

As Gramma approached the looming outline of the butte, she veered to the right, just as the regular path did, and skirted it. A short ten minutes later brought her to the riverbank where fifty-six years earlier she had begun creating images with words snatched from the ether of her mind. In absolute darkness now, the truck's headlights created two bright spotlights on the slowly flowing river water. Leaving the engine running, she pushed the gear lever forward into park, and then straining with both hands, managed to set the handbrake. Carefully she climbed out of the massive truck and lowered herself to the ground. She walked down to the water's edge and, peering right and left, saw no sign of her granddaughter. She cupped her hands around her mouth and mustering all her vocal power, shouted downstream in the direction the water flowed, "Kate! Yoo-hoo, Kate Flannery!"

She waited ten silent seconds for a response, then upstream, repeated her desperate call. She strained her ears for a faint cry for help, but the soft coo of gentle water seeking a lower place, and the steady heartbeat of the Ford's engine behind her were all she heard. She glanced up, and thousands of feet above her, a big jet heading west out of O'Hare International in Chicago sliced through the shimmering light of uncountable stars, bound for some faraway destination.

A tremendous need to weep surged through Gramma just as she heard the rustle of powerful wings beside her. "Oh, Orville," she sobbed, "where can our Kate be?" Somehow, Orville's presence reassured her. She gulped back the tears and wiped her nose on the sleeve of her jacket.

"If I wait here, will you fly down the river a mile or so and see if you can spot her? I don't know how well you can see in the dark, but please examine along the banks. She's such a strong swimmer, Orville. I'm certain she's okay. And do be careful—fly safely. It's sure to be terribly risky for you now the sun's gone down."

Orville had no time to explain about his eyesight and didn't wait for further instructions. Immediately, he rose and began to skim downstream barely ten feet off the water. His vision was pure now; with absolute darkness came perfect clarity and sharp as honed steel depth perception. Each watery ripple, frosted frothy white by fresh starlight, became distinct as if it were a jagged mountaintop in the snow-covered Himalayan range in distant Kashmir.

The algebra of the search was also perfectly clear: $D = vt$ where D is distance, v is velocity, and t is time. If the river flows at three miles per hour, and Kate has been missing almost three hours, then, unconscious and floating with the current, she could be as far as nine miles hence. Confident of his calculations, Orville sped headlong downstream into the slumbering night.

Chapter Seventeen
No Angels in Sight

At the Academy, part of Higgins's training was called "Water Survival and the Mind." Since outstanding red-tails from all over America are recruited to enroll there, the training must be appropriate for all geographical locations, not just those found in South Dakota. At the conclusion of the first day, Higgins's homework assignment was a passage from a military study done of World War II aviators and Navy survivors at sea.

Just before class was adjourned for the day, the instructor, a slim stately hawk from Cardiff, Wales, Professor RT Cedric Shinned, posed the following question: "Lads, does age have anything to do with a man's ability to survive for a prolonged period in the water?"

The answer seemed perfectly obvious to Higgins. Several of his more eloquent classmates volunteered their opinions: younger, stronger men would almost certainly outlast their older shipmates in such a situation. Turns out, they were all dead wrong. The research, much to their surprise, revealed older, more mature aviators and sailors, despite their comparative lack of youthful strength, survived at a higher rate than their younger shipmates.

What could cause such an illogical conclusion? The younger men, it seems, even though physically stronger, gave up hope of being rescued sooner and allowed themselves to slip into their watery graves. The older men, though desperately exhausted, were somehow able to dig deeper into their core willpower and hang on long enough to be rescued.

The young hawks in training took the lesson to heart. Thankfully, Higgins had never had occasion to put it to the test.

The sky over the well was pitch-black, softened by a faint swath of sparkling diamonds in the Milky Way. The sky in the well, without benefit of starlight, loomed darker than the inside of a murderer's skull. Kate shuddered and wondered if her eyes were open or shut. From time to time she pulled her now wrinkled hands out of the water and vigorously rubbed her face just to make certain.

It had been over five hours since she had fallen into the well, though she couldn't see her wristwatch even if she cared to track the time. Her lips had long ago turned blue, and for the first two hours her teeth chattered incessantly. Next, wall-to-wall goose bumps arrived, and the uncontrollable, constant shaking similar to the shuddering palsy of a fevered malaria patient in a steamy jungle prisoner of war camp came calling, before an over-all numbness took hold and forced Kate's defensive mechanisms to be still.

She backed herself against one wall and let her head loll against it as a sort of resting place. Mostly she stood flat-footed with her chin just out of the water, but from time to time she flexed her left leg, went up on the toes of her foot, waved her arms underwater and bobbed for a minute or two.

Beginning when she was seven Kate had taken six weeks of swimming lessons down at Dupree every summer and had easily progressed from Pollywog to Dolphin at the end of her training. She had been invited to become an instructor when she turned sixteen, which she intended to do. To Kate Flannery, water had always been a safe, friendly, and fun element—certainly not one to fear.

But there was plenty in the darkness to fear. It was a smothering black and it caught in her throat, making it difficult to breathe. It was nightmarishly dark, yet she knew she was not dreaming.

During the sixth hour of her immersion her mind wandered to stories she had read.

She remembered her favorite chapter in *The Hobbit*. It was titled "Riddles in the Dark" and concerned the hobbit, Bilbo Baggins, being lost far underground until he blindly waded into a seemingly bottomless lake inhabited by a slimy creature named Gollum. After a terrifying encounter with the watery monster, Baggins eventually escaped back to the light of day. In recalling this incident, Kate drew strength for herself. Surely her present ordeal was not any worse than the hobbit's had been. She felt the corners of her mouth wrinkle into an invisible grin.

Even so, a certain untamed fear remained and horrid ideas seeped, uninvited, into her thoughts. What would happen if the well caved in on her? She quickly dismissed the thought of being buried alive, but nonetheless it kept simmering on the back burners of her restless mind.

And what if no one could find the well? She knew the cover was overgrown with prairie grass and nearly undetectable. How many hours would it be before she would fall asleep and let herself sink under the surface? Grasping for dwindling hope, she refused to consider it.

Her mind skipped to a time, three years earlier, when her grandfather was still alive. The entire family had taken a long, three-day weekend getaway trip and driven clear to Sioux Falls. There had been a carnival in town, and Kate had stood on the balcony of their motel room watching a huge beacon of light sweep the night sky, advertising the carnival's presence.

Mesmerized, Kate had begged her parents to take her there. Holding hands, three generations of the Flannery family had walked the midway together, dazzled by the flashing lights, raucous sounds, and tempting smells of the glitzy carnival. They stuffed handfuls of sugary fluffs of pink cotton candy into their laughing mouths; the wonderful aroma of sizzling onion burgers forced them to sit, eat, and rest; they rode high above the city on the spidery arms of the Ferris wheel, and pitched thin dimes at tiny, slippery saucers.

Somehow Grampa Ernie, against all odds, had flipped a dime into the air and when it struck a saucer, it bounced once and clung to the surface. He had won a long purple snake for his prize, and Kate, pretending to be strangling, had wrapped it gleefully around her neck.

An hour later as they departed through the main entrance, Kate's eyes were drawn like marauding mosquitoes to the heat and brilliance of the giant, mirrored-glass searchlight. Peering upward into the firmament, her mouth gaping wide with wonder, she could see the magnified light bouncing off skittering clouds—creating an eerie, almost heavenly vision.

Grampa Flannery, noticing Kate's upward gaze had remarked, "See any angels up there, Kate? I do." Ten months later, her beloved grandfather had taken his assigned place to perch with the angels.

Back now to the well's silent darkness, her wrinkled hand probed until it found the pack's zipper, and with uncertain fingers managed to draw it down until she could slide her hand inside. She slowly pried the coffee can lid off and reaching inside, gripped her tiny flashlight. With considerable effort she raised both arms out of the water. Carefully she twisted one end of the flashlight and was instantly rewarded with a thin beam of comforting light directed uncertainly against the side of the well.

Now she raised her arm and pointed the insignificant beacon directly overhead and through the hole above her; seeking help, the light fled out into the distant heavens. How long, she wondered, would it take for the light's beam to reach the distant stars and bounce back? Would frantic searchers be drawn to the light like heat-seeking insects to the lights of a summer porch on a pleasant summer evening? Dare Kate hope for such a doubtful miracle?

A long minute passed. Her wavering arm grew tired and so she switched the flashlight to her left hand. Clumsy numbness took over; her deft touch failed, and the little firefly flashlight, her one beacon of hope, plunged into the water and drowned itself. Once again, Kate had seen no angels.

During the next hour, to help the time pass more quickly and to keep herself company, she began to talk out loud. "I'm sure Gramma has called Mom in Rapid City by now." The sound of her voice in the hideous darkness was somehow reassuring.

"It takes a little over four hours to drive from there back home. I hope Dad doesn't drive too fast and get a ticket for speeding. I know he'll be mad at me for not staying on the path. He'll probably ground me for the rest of my life. Who cares? I'll be alive and out of this hole. When they get home they'll drive straight to the river, and when they don't find me there, Dad will begin searching next to the trail in each direction until he finds the well. It's not likely he can see it in the dark even with his big flashlight, so he'll probably start again in the morning as soon as light's up."

Kate refused to acknowledge the distinct possibility her father or any other searcher might accidentally step on the camouflaged well cover and tumble down on top of her.

"Knowing Dad, he'll discover where I walked up the butte, then down the other side and eventually he'll follow my tracks right to the well. He's always got ropes and stuff in the truck so he can fish me out easy enough. All I have to do is stay awake and be patient."

These voiced words of optimism were a bulwark against the constant gnawing fear. She was almost certain now, with the morning light, she would be pulled to safety.

In Rapid City, Kate's parents had just polished off a scrumptious steak dinner in the Rusty Spurs restaurant, a few deserted blocks from their motel. As they strolled back, Dave's big rough hand gently engulfed his wife's small soft one.

Beth Flannery, responding to Dave's love and tenderness, leaned her head against his strong shoulder, gazed upward at the cloudless firmament, and observed, "Aren't the stars beautiful tonight?"

Chapter Eighteen
Disaster Strikes

*O*RVILLE'S NORMAL SUSTAINED POINT A TO point B daytime flight speed was a near constant thirty miles per hour, somewhat below average for a young male red-tail. Because his vision was never reliable in the daylight hours, he always deliberately flew a few notches below his potential top speed. However at night, with his extra-large pupils gaping wide and the terrain below him laser clear, he cruised closer to thirty-eight and when the situation demanded it, could punch it up to forty, even forty-five.

Simple algebra told him $T = d/v$—where the time he needed to fly was equal to the distance (nine miles) divided by his average flight speed velocity (thirty-eight miles per hour). Doing the calculations rapidly in his mind, he converted the time to minutes and realized he would cover the total nine-mile distance in just over fourteen minutes.

With the Ford's lights shining brightly in the water behind him, Orville checked his Breitling Aviator wing watch at 21:34. All South Dakota red-tails who graduate from flight school are required to use military time and after graduation, out of habit, often continue to use it the rest of their lives. It was 9:34 in the evening.

Fourteen minutes later, at 21:48, just as the dotted lights of the small settlement of Iron Lightning came into view, Orville banked sharply and immediately began the return trip. He'd seen nothing of note save a few deer cautiously drinking at the river's edge.

When he arrived back at the truck, landing with a light thump on the passenger side mirror, Gramma was wrapped in a blanket she had found stuffed behind the seat of the truck. The Ford's engine was still idling and she was seated behind the steering wheel with the heater going full blast.

She fumbled for the window button and zipped the glass down. She leaned across the gear shifter toward the open window and said, "Will you please come in here, Orville? It's freezing out there."

Without unfolding his wings he merely fluffed his tail feathers and leaped unceremoniously from the mirror post through the open window, landing on the passenger seat next to Gramma. In the process his cast had banged against the window frame and he winced with a quick, sharp stab of pain in his broken leg. The effort of skimming over the twisting river for eighteen miles, nine down and back, had his heart pounding and blood racing. The blower on the heater ruffled the feathers around his face and he immediately felt uncomfortably warm.

Gramma had draped part of the blanket over her head and held it closed under her chin with her left hand, giving her somewhat the appearance of a carefree Goldilocks skipping through the forest to grandmother's house. She reached over with her right hand and caressed Orville's head, smoothing out his ruffled feathers.

"I assume you didn't find Kate or you wouldn't be back here so soon," she said. "How could she just disappear into thin air, Orville? It's simply not possible for her to vanish like this. I'm so cold I can't think straight anymore. I wish I had called Beth and Dave straight away. It's all my fault." She stopped rambling and holding both hands up to her face sobbed softly into a wad of Kleenex.

Orville sat quietly, trying to puzzle out the possibilities. He was now absolutely certain Kate was not in or near the river. He was also positive she was not on the trail they had traveled together earlier in the day, nor had she taken a detour route around the butte to the west. Logic assured him unless she had somehow come in contact with another human being who had dragged her away against her will, she had to be somewhere between the butte and the ranch house.

Just then Gramma calmed down, caught her breath, and dabbing at her eyes and nose, said, "Orv, the best thing to do now is drive back home and call Dave. He'll know what to do. I only pray it's not too late."

Orville had just decided to fly a grid he'd mapped out in his mind. It would be the classic hunting technique of red-tails: soaring in a tight circle near the center of a target area, and then gradually widening each orbit until the entire area had been closely scrutinized. It was the exact technique he'd been flying the day he'd crashed into the Flannery ranch house. His accident though, had occurred in bright sunlight when his eyesight had been compromised.

Orville realized he would need to cover a rectangular area roughly three miles long and no more than two miles wide. He had already selected a starting point about a half-mile south of the butte, equidistant between the river and the Flannery's home. If need be he was prepared to scour every inch of land between the ranch house and the river.

With the river directly in front of her and no convenient spot to turn the big truck around, Gramma, teeth wildly chattering, stared up at the rearview mirror so she could see through the rear window of the truck's cab, released the parking brake, and mistakenly pulled the shift lever out of park and into drive. She felt the gears mesh, slid her toe off the brake, mashed the gas pedal, and the truck lurched wildly forward down the riverbank and into the river.

Orville, surprised by the sudden roar of the engine and the lunge down the riverbank, was thrown catawampus off the slippery seat and onto the floor of the passenger side. He landed awkwardly and just before impact instinctively threw both legs down to cushion the blow. A searing bolt of pain jolted his broken leg and momentarily robbed him of breath; his body began to spasm uncontrollably, the result of a quick frisson of agony. Not wanting to alarm Gramma even more, he clamped his beak shut, throttling the cry of pain deep in his throat.

Meanwhile, Gramma, mortified at the mistake she had made, rammed the truck's shifter into reverse and stomped on the gas pedal. The wheels spun viciously in the sandy river bottom, and the Ford gave it a valiant try, but without solid traction, didn't move. The weight of the engine in the front anchored the truck where it was while the rear end, lighter and partially buoyant, swung slowly around and began to drift downstream, making it appear the truck was being driven upstream against the current.

The initial impetus of their charge down the bank and into the river had landed them near the middle of four feet of serenely flowing water. In a moment the engine sputtered, coughed twice, and fell silent. The depth of the river partially covered the headlights, creating an eerie underwater glow like the lights from an underwater village seen at night.

"Orville," Gramma cried, "we've got to get out! Hurry!"

Panicked, she put her bony shoulder to the door and it swung stubbornly open against the river flow. Immediately the partially open door allowed the slow moving water to cascade over the door's threshold and into the truck's cab. Instinctively Gramma lifted her feet so as to not get her shoes wet. Too late!

She pulled the blanket off her shoulders, leaned far to her right and roughly plucked the suffering Orville from the floor where he was grimly floating like an unhappy cat being bathed in a backyard tub. Bracing her left knee against the door to keep it open, she held him out over the river with both hands and tossed him like an old-fashioned, two-handed free-throw attempt, into the air.

"Fly," she commanded, as if she were a determined mother hawk forcing her timid nestling over the dizzying precipice of their nest for the first time.

Orville, caught in the cruel vise of woe, nevertheless opened his wings, caught air, fanned his tail, and soundlessly fluttered the short distance to shore. Despite being wet and consumed with the white-hot flames of pain racking his tortured leg, he managed to land safely without causing any further damage. Trying desperately to catch his heaving breath, he turned his attention back to the river.

Meanwhile, Gramma had gathered her dress high above her waist and stepped barelegged into the river. The cold water made her gasp, and unsure of the depth, she stumbled, almost falling headlong into the current. To prevent herself from losing her balance completely and going under, she let go of her balled up dress and threw her arms out to the sides.

She was drenched now, and little to be done about it. Holding the door open with her backside, she leaned into the truck and grabbed the blanket off the seat, carrying it bunched up on her head, safely out of the water. She braced her thin legs against the moving water, and once steadied, allowed the current to slam the truck door shut, but not before a foot or so of the Moreau River had filled the bottom of the driver's compartment, stopping just short of the seat bottoms.

Abandoning the truck, with the headlights still casting an unnatural glow on the river's surface, she waded ashore, twisting her hips forcefully from side to side, much like a leggy New York fashion model strutting herself down a glowing runway.

Crying openly now, she climbed the bank to where Orville sat, perched on his good leg. "I've made such a horrid mess of things," she sputtered. "Stupid, stupid me." Gramma opened the dry blanket and wrapped it over her head and shoulders. The dress, soaked clear to her chest, clung heavily to her body and shivering legs.

She bent over and gently picked up Orville; wrapping her shaking arms around him, she held him to her cheek in a loving embrace like a mother shielding her infant from a fierce cold wind. Fortunately for Gramma, darkness hid the steady trickle of warm crimson seeping onto the blanket, sparing her the knowledge of Orville's grievous injury. His plaster cast could not begin to contain the rush of fresh blood.

Orville manacled his beak by will alone, and did not moan.

Chapter Nineteen
Thanks Be To Pandora

WHILE A STUDENT AT THE ACADEMY IN PIERRE, Higgins was required to attend a weekly lecture on Greek Mythology. The forum was held every Saturday morning at zero eight hundred hours, a most horrible time for young bachelor cadets to convene for serious contemplation. He had few distinct recollections of the sober weekly gatherings except one: the Greek myth concerning Pandora. Apparently Pandora was the first woman on earth, and she embraced a pithos or storage jar holding captive all the miseries of mankind—greed, vanity, slander, envy, and pining.

The cadets, those able to keep their drowsy eyes and ears open, learned Pandora's name means all gifts, and the jar contained her dowry. She was warned Zeus forbade her to ever open the jar, but curiosity eventually overpowered her, and one day she popped off the lid—allowing all the miseries inside to break out and forevermore trouble the world. As luck would have it though, Pandora was able to slam the lid shut just before the last element escaped.

It was this ethereal substance Kate Flannery so desperately needed.

Kate awoke choking with a mouth full of stale water. How long she had dozed she wasn't sure. The well and the blackness above and below her were perfectly silent, and there was no indication dawn would soon appear. Or, horror of horrors, had it already appeared, and like a missed final train, gone again while she slept?

She was surprised she hadn't heard any sounds of a search party. On TV when searches for lost people were mounted there were always hovering helicopters with blazing searchlights and dozens of emergency vehicles with flashing red and blue lights scattered about. She had watched news clips of uniformed men chasing after leashed dogs while they searched for lost children. But here in the well, she could hear no such rescue commotion—no throbbing copter blades, no wailing sirens, no barking dogs—just barren silence.

Long ago she had let her arms droop to her sides in the water, and from the chin down she might as well have been paralyzed. She no longer felt pain, nor cold, nor thirst, nor hunger. The water and layered darkness, like a merciful dose of morphine to someone in the last few days of hospice care, had somehow muted those natural mechanisms. Like an unborn fetus cushioned by the amniotic fluid in her mother's uterus, Kate was slowly returning whence she began.

Was she beginning to hallucinate? She blinked her eyes, not knowing whether they were shut or open. Was she hearing unspoken sounds? A school hallway, near the entrance to the cafeteria appeared before her. She spun the dial of her combination lock and her locker door tumbled open, fell off its rusty hinges, clattered to the floor at her feet. She swung her backpack, heavily laden with schoolbooks, and let it drop into the cavernous locker.

Hearing mocking laughter approaching, she half turned. A hand pushed her chest. Three girls taunted her; she recognized their faces, pouty mouths garishly lipsticked, black eyes outlined with white powder, but couldn't remember their names. One spoke: "Well here she is—Little Miss Straight A Kate herself. Kissed any teacher butt today, Miss Perfect?"

Kate backed up, stumbled, and fell over her locker door, landing with an embarrassing and painful thump. The three tormenters jabbed at her with dagger-like bright red fingernails. "You are disgusting," they said in unison, then laughed hysterically.

Kate tried to crawl away, but they began to chant: "Brown nose! Brown nose! What Kate Flannery kisses, everybody knows!" A curious crowd of onlookers had gathered. Some joined the three girls, jeering, pointing, and chanting, while others, frowning in obvious embarrassment or shame, remained silent—and yet no one came forward to help.

"Brown nose! Brown nose!" The vile words rang in her ears.

With a start, Kate raised her hands out of the water as if to ward off the girls and snapped back to her senses. Though numb, she sobbed. The tears soon subsided, and a series of soft whimpers, unheeded cries for mercy, replaced the choked sobs.

In the dark a vision came to her: On the tattered hem of Dupree's outskirts, across the railroad tracks and past the river, lay the town cemetery. The oldest and largest monuments, some leaning precariously, were closest to the narrow, winding dirt road circling through the gravesites. Four or five ancient oak trees scattered here and there offered scant shade. One had been struck by lightning some time ago, and bereft of life, pointed the way upward with a sharp snag of a fleshless arm, slicing through the sky toward heaven.

Last Memorial Day, Kate had gotten down on her knees and slowly snipped her way around the small, polished granite marker of her grandfather's grave with grass clippers, while the rest of the Flannery family had stood nearby. Just before they walked back to the car for the drive home, Gramma knelt and laid a bouquet of freshly cut spring flowers on her husband's grave, and then, without warning, she rolled onto her back in the untended grass a few feet away.

Shading her eyes with one hand Gramma said to her family, the dead oak tree also bearing witness, "When my turn comes, put me here next to him. We can listen to the rain together."

From the blackness of the well, Kate saw a new marker, the piled South Dakota dirt still tinted orange with freshness. Etched into the cold hunk of granite were the words:

Katherine Susan Flannery
Born September 10, 1999
Died August 28, 2012
Our daughter, Kate. Oh! What a girl!

Kate's body sagged, and she allowed herself to die. She took a final breath, went under. Is this how you drown? The thought came to her unbidden, and she remembered during the free swim time after the lessons were complete at the pool in Dupree, the kids sometimes held their breath for as long as possible while letting themselves float face down in the water without moving a muscle. They called it the dead man's float and thought it was hilarious.

Kate willed herself to blow out the meager breath of air saved in her mouth. It bubbled to the surface and now less buoyant, she sank limply—a dead girl's float. As if detached from her body, she felt one knee graze the slimy bottom. The blood began to pound in her ears, and she saw brilliant sparks of red and orange and white flare behind her eyes. Her lungs screamed for just one more breath of life.

Too close to suicide, Kate was unable to bear death this way, and she kicked out hard. Her left foot hit something solid, propelled her, and porpoise-like she exploded to the surface gasping for precious air; it filled her lungs, forced oxygen to her limbs, renewed her courage to face whatever deadly perils lay ahead.

Kate, momentarily re-energized, let her restless mind meander. What, she wondered, had happened to Orville when he arrived home carrying her fishing pole? Had Gramma even noticed his return? Had he eventually grown weary of waiting for her to return from the river and finally winged off to his real home somewhere in a tall tree rooted beside a creek bed out on the prairie?

Would she ever see him again? Surely he wouldn't abandon her. Did he have a cute hawk friend somewhere, or a lonely, loving mate high in a tree warming two eggs in their nest?

If so, surely Orville's wife would be worried about his prolonged absence. Perhaps he had heeded her call to return to his family.

Kate vaguely remembered a vehicle and a cloud of dust she had seen while resting on top of the butte before she had plunged into the well. Had she just imagined it, or was it possible something terrible had happened to Gramma, and she had called for the doctor to come out to the house? What if Gramma had suffered a stroke and was unable to speak, or had fallen unconscious? She wouldn't be able to explain Kate was missing. No one would know until her parents returned home Sunday evening and couldn't locate her.

Her thoughts wandered on a new path, back toward the ranch house. Kate could see the house enveloped by the night, lights ablaze. Inside, her mother poured steaming coffee into thick mugs. The kitchen was crowded with big-shouldered men. Her father's best friend in high school, Ben Dredge, now the sheriff of Ziebach County, and several other impressive uniformed officers, crowded around the Flannery kitchen table.

Sheriff Dredge pointed his thick forefinger at a wrinkled map, spoke loudly, and the other men bent over, studying the map intently. Her father said something Kate couldn't hear and they all turned simultaneously and stared at the big clock on the kitchen wall. Kate could not read the time and the second hand seemed to be moving counterclockwise. Had time already ended for her? It was a horrifying thought.

Below the clock her mother stood, a renegade wisp of hair fell from her forehead and covered one eye. She fretfully tucked it behind her ear, then wiped her hands on a kitchen towel. A mounded plate of sliced banana bread still warm from the oven was handed from man to man. Lips pulled tight, they nibbled, sipped coffee, and turned back to the map.

Once again, Kate somehow dispatched a reluctant messenger from her brain to her knees. The knees slowly unlocked, and her body sagged slightly this time. She took a big breath, gave herself permission to dip her head under the water for a brief second or two then she reversed the process, straightened her back, locked the linchpin in her knees, and emerged again. Momentarily refreshed, Kate blinked her eyes rapidly and looked again for the clock on the wall, but the kitchen had vanished—the house, her mother, her father, and the uniformed men—gone—empty, dark, nothing.

She must try her best to keep her head above water and wait. She bristled with a brief burst of confidence. She had already met the demons of darkness and fear; she had tasted their poison—and spat it out, felt their sting—and rubbed it off. Sooner or later the loyal dawn would arrive, and even a tiny sliver of light from the hole above her would be warming and welcome. She sensed if she could hold on just a few hours more, somehow witness another daybreak, her rescue would be imminent.

Kate stubbornly clung to the idea. She braced her back against the side of the well, gathered courage, and peered upward. It seemed to her the shade of darkness hovering near the lid of her trap was a tiny bit lighter.

A bit of inspiration came to her. She willed her shriveled arms out of the water and snaked her right hand through the strap of her floating backpack. Pulling it to her chest she managed to get her left arm through the other strap. The pack, buoyed by the air trapped in the coffee can and the two water bottles, bobbed lightly in front of her face. Locking her fingers together behind the pack she had created, minimal though it might be, what the U.S. Coast Guard refers to as an improvised flotation device, though Kate knew nothing of such terms.

Gratefully she allowed her head to droop forward and rest on the pack. Wearily she closed her eyes. After a few seconds her eyes flickered open and without raising her head, she snarled in defiance, her teeth bared like a cornered animal: "I am not going to give up. I won't die in this awful place."

Kate, certain the darkness seeping into and consuming every molecule of her being was not quite as black as before, whispered through bloated, yet hopeful lips, "Hurry, Dad. Please hurry."

Pandora's box—after all misery was emptied from it— still contained hope.

Chapter Twenty
Risky Business

HIGGINS CONSIDERED HIMSELF FAIRLY WELL read and capable of understanding much of the world, but some things remained beyond his intellectual capacity—primarily ancient geological, astronomical, and anthropological events.

Eminent scientists the world over believe planet Earth is billions of years old. It has, at various times, been covered in amazingly deep ice, and tens of thousands of years ago the ice melted away and tropical forests emerged and flourished. Unbelievably huge animals walked about and enormous birds skittered through the air. Massive meteors and comets slammed into earth with force enough to darken the sky and choke the air with impenetrable dust. Land, once mountainous, became submerged to terrible depths in great seas while earthquakes and volcanoes of terrific magnitude rent the earth and forged magnificent mountain ranges.

Higgins had been taught these histories and didn't doubt them for a moment, yet his mind could not grasp them fully. Despite these cataclysmic, earth-shattering events, the exquisitely delicate butterfly, the gossamer petals of the orchid, and diaphanous winged hummingbirds, his diminutive cousins, were somehow spared destruction, and live yet. These ideas were too distant, too gigantic, and too wondrous for the teacher to comprehend.

The Moreau River carves a roundabout channel nearly halfway across the state of South Dakota. It begins innocently enough high in the Rocky Mountains almost to Wyoming in the west and slowly wends its way east, until it eventually empties into Lake Oahe and the Missouri River. Higgins could not begin to fathom how many millions of years it had taken for the flowing water to etch itself into the plains. Or, he sometimes wondered, had it happened in just one explosive day?

In Higgins's dream he was much younger. He had zeroed in on a squirrel and was about to begin his descent when a murder of crows interrupted his quest. The crows were enormous, almost eagle-sized, and their caws were ear-splitting roars of defiant challenge. His wings felt ponderously heavy, barely responding to his need for valiant speed. Black wings fiendishly buffeted him, and wickedly snapping beaks tore at his flesh. He held his breath and rolled into the almost suicidal *Open Coffin Spin* maneuver to escape, letting out a desperate wail for help.

The incessant ringing of the phone jarred him awake, rescuing him from his own subconscious fears. His pajamas were soaked with sweat and he glanced quickly at the luminous dial of the bedside clock—zero two hundred hours. Who could be calling at such an obscene hour of the night?

"Higgins." His voice was thick with sleep, his mind still clanging with devilish images of hateful crows.

"Dr. Higgins?"

"Yes, yes. Who's calling please?"

"This is Annabelle Matthews. Your former student? I'm so sorry to trouble you in the middle of the night, Higgins, sir, but something terrible has happened."

Higgins snapped alert. "No trouble at all, young hawk. It's good to hear from you, Annabelle. How may I help?"

"Earlier this evening, just at dusk, I was cruising home from a hunt east of Iron Lightning when I heard an appalling cry for help."

"Hawk, or...?"

"Human, sir. It was a piteous scream and I haven't been able to sleep tonight because of it. I live alone and can't get it out of my mind. Sorry to wake you, sir."

"Please just call me Boyd, Annabelle. No need of 'sir.' I'm your friend now, not your flight instructor." He paused, trying to organize his thoughts. "What happened to the person who screamed?"

"That's the weird part, Higgins, sir. I mean, Boyd, sir. The shriek penetrated my airspace and beyond, yet there was not a living soul in sight. I scoured the ground below me, but there was absolutely no one about. And yet, I'm certain I heard a scream."

"Were you able to discern male or female?"

"It was high-pitched and youthful, sir. I'm almost positive it was a young girl."

"What were your coordinates above the scream?"

"As usual I was flying at six hundred and fifty feet. When I circled back I marked at 45.2 degrees north and 101.8 degrees west, sir. I double-checked the time on my Breitling and the setting sun off the horizon. My watch is precise to the second."

"Roughly a mile south of the Moreau River and about ten miles west of Iron Lightning village, isn't it?" Higgins slipped out of bed and pulled back the curtains on the bedroom window. The view faced out to the east and there was not yet the barest hint of approaching dawn.

"Almost exactly. It's right adjacent to a place in the river called Dahl's Bend. If you recall, sir, we held our senior class picnic there. Remember Yancy and Horatio got into a dust up over the last hotdog? Oh, one other thing. I did note a Chicago Cubs baseball cap on the ground nearby."

"Nothing else?" Higgins was having difficulty wrapping his mind around the mystery of a baffling scream and cap, but no person.

"No one around at all, sir. After dinner I couldn't shake the feeling someone needed help, and I've been tossing and turning about it all night. Haven't slept a wink. It's too dark to fly safely now, sir, but at first light I'm going back for a closer look, unless you've got a better idea."

"Do you remember the red-tails' creed, Annabelle?"

"Indeed, sir. 'Never kill beyond need. Always help beyond the asking.'" She giggled into the phone. "You made us recite the creed every morning for nine months. I'll never forget it, sir."

"If someone out there truly needs help, Annabelle, we can't postpone our flight until it's a safe and convenient hour. Give me ten minutes to get ready and another twenty minutes to fly." He grabbed his Breitling wingwatch off the bedside table and held it up to his straining eyes. "Let's see. I've got exactly zero two sixteen now, so let's rendezvous at zero two forty-six, over the river at Dahl's Bend. We can proceed from there to the baseball cap, and then I can follow you down. I'm sure your eyes are much better in the dark than mine. Sound okay?"

"Yes, sir. I'm already dressed and ready to go out the door. Do be careful, Higgins, sir. It's quite risky business."

"See you soon, Annabelle." He put the phone down softly in its cradle. He chuckled at her final comment. The young flyer was concerned about the old flyer crashing in the dark.

It was then he recalled the note Annabelle's junior high teacher had placed in her student file all those years ago—*I worry she lacks confidence and will not take the fight to the prey. How false those penned words have proven to be,* he thought, *and perhaps a good lesson for teachers to consider before labeling their students.*

Twisting every which way, he managed to cinch the strap on his wing holster. "I've trained her well," he murmured. He pondered again her parting: "Do be careful, Higgins, sir. It's quite risky business."

A wide smile slid across his face. "Indeed it is, Annabelle. Quite a dangerous undertaking. And thus the world has always been."

Chapter Twenty-one
An Ordeal Begins

Fortunately for Gramma her jacket had gotten wet only at the waistband, and her ancient Cubs cap had not been lost in the river.

"Excuse me, Orville," she said through chattering teeth, "but I've got to get this wet dress off before I freeze to death. Don't peek."

Tenderly, she lowered Orville to the ground where he perched unsteadily on his one good leg. Gramma quickly unzipped her jacket and dropped it and her cap on the bank. Reaching behind her back with numb fingers, she clumsily groped for the zipper to her dress. It eluded her. Exasperated, she quickly pulled the dress up to her face, and with great effort forced her head through the narrow opening. She heard a tearing sound, and then it was off. Her pearl-colored satin slip, also soaked, slid off much easier.

Clad now in bra and panties, she bent over and quickly donned her jacket again. Then she picked up her cap and like a submarine sailor standing on the boat's deck in a gale, pulled it down almost to her ears with a hard yank on the bill. Bending over again, she gave the blanket a quick shake, and then wrapped it sarong-like around her narrow hips, covering her shivering and blanched white legs. Struggling with numb fingertips, she finally tied off two corners of the blanket at the waist to secure it.

"At least now I'm dry, Orville. I think I can walk home from here. No doubt there's a flashlight in the glove box, but I'm not going back in the river to fetch it. Anyway, I've walked home from here a thousand times and know the way by heart. There's plenty of starlight to light my way. I'll call Dave at the hotel as soon as I get back home. There's no time to waste. Let's go."

Her thin white socks and canvas sneakers were soaked and squished some with each step, but with her positive words came positive action. She strode briskly toward home.

The biological miracle of clotting had stemmed the flow of blood from Orville's damaged leg, and the pain had lessened to the point it was no longer a hindrance. From his resting spot he briefly inspected the cast and though it had changed in color from a dirty white to almost black with crusted blood, it would have to do until he could fly to Dupree and have Doc Walters reset the bone.

He wasn't quite sure how the truck had ended up in the river, but the sight of it mired there now, lights still blazing under water, made him grin despite his fresh injury. In the Prairie Winds classroom Orville had read Shakespeare's *A Midsummer Night's Dream* out loud together with his classmates and had fallen in love with the mischievous character, Puck.

In particular, Orville was astonished at Puck's spectacular flying ability, capable of putting "a girdle round about the earth in forty minutes," and his humorous pranks against the humans. And, when Puck proclaimed, "Lord, what fools these mortals be," the class had laughed and laughed, their funny bones severely tickled.

Those ancient words of mirth resonated in Orville's mind now when he thought of Gramma accidentally driving the truck down the bank and plunging headlong into the river.

With a start, Orville realized Gramma had already been swallowed by the darkness and he swiftly launched himself, gained a bit of altitude and circled fifty feet or so over her head. He watched carefully as she sloshed slowly along, holding her makeshift sarong tightly with one hand. He could see she was safely on course and in no immediate danger so he soared even higher, until he reached the optimum surveillance height of six hundred fifty feet.

The butte, still a mile to the south, was the sole distinctive feature in the entire landscape. Carefully considering the situation once more, he reasoned if a walking person became lost in this wide-open area, it would be reasonable to assume the butte would most likely have something to do with it. Directly over the butte now, he began his reconnaissance with a small circle pattern with a diameter of no more than fifty feet, just a constant tight turn for a red-tail.

Nearly two miles off in the distance to the south, he could see the glowing light on the Flannery home's back porch and a rectangular block of light blazing through the kitchen window.

Glancing toward Gramma he saw her journey was progressing, though for some reason, it seemed to have slowed. He hesitated to leave the formal flight grid to check on her. She had already walked perhaps three fourths of a mile and was approaching the point in the path where it veered east to the side of the butte.

Gradually the circumference of his circle patterns increased until he flew about four hundred yards to complete the loop. As he banked his wings toward the river, he noticed a pile of bricks lying in disarray along with some weathered boards. Could Kate have tangled herself under those boards somehow? It seemed preposterous to him, but glancing down to make certain Gramma was still walking true along the path, he decided to quickly inspect the site.

He dove silently through the night, slowed, and landed with a soft thump. He perched one-legged on a jumbled section of Björn Dahl's ruined fireplace, elevated off the ground about three bricks high, which had not yet fully crumbled to the ground. Straining his ears for the slightest of abnormal sounds, he heard nothing unusual. His eyes scoured the surrounding area, and then his heart skipped a beat.

Kate's baseball cap! Surely it was! She had come this way. There was no doubt about it. Just then he heard Gramma's voice.

"Orville. Do come here, if you will."

Quickly he elevated and winged swiftly toward her call. When he arrived she was bent over and down on one knee adjusting a shoe. He voiced a soft klrrr-klrrr-klrrr, *'Tis but I,* so she would not be overly startled by his sudden presence.

"I'm getting a bad blister on my heel from this shoe slipping up and down on my wet sock," she said. "Makes it most difficult to walk."

Orville was pleased to hear the rhyme from her, though her usual careful attention to meter was way off. *Rhyming even while in pain has to be a positive sign,* he thought. He wanted to comfort her, but knew she had at least two more miles to walk, and blisters or not, she would just have to tough it out. Paramount in his mind at the moment was to return to Kate's cap and evaluate the situation there. It was a mystery he trusted could be easily unraveled.

Gramma said, "Hopefully, I'll be home soon, with or without old man moon. Don't worry 'bout me. I'm good as can be." She clenched her teeth and trudging forward, winced now with each painful step.

Orville admired her stubborn determination, but said nothing. He sat quietly considering the possibilities.

Once Gramma left his field of vision as the trail bent around the butte, he once more launched himself, headed in the direction of the Cubs baseball cap. This time he glided to a near perfect landing beside it. To his horror he perceived a dark hole in the earth, just the perfect size for Kate's slender shoulders to slide through. Gingerly holding his injured leg out to the side, he hopped crow-like to the edge, peered in and, tilting his head, listened with all his might.

His heart leapt with joy as he heard the same sounds of peaceful slumber he had grown accustomed to while sleeping beside Kate's bed. He couldn't be positive, but her breathing seemed slightly shallower and more rapid. *Surely not a good sign,* he thought.

Careful not to lose his one-legged balance, he craned his neck over the edge as far as he dared. Far below he could make out the top of Kate's head, long strands of her blond, floating braid trailing out behind. Both gladdened and alarmed, and not fully realizing Kate was being inexorably tugged, minute-by-minute, closer to death, he winged off toward Gramma.

Gramma's legs wobbled as she barely shuffled forward. Dark stains on both heels gave mute testimony to her suffering, yet she forced herself up the long driveway from the main road to the back porch.

Never before in fifty-six years of life spent in Ziebach County had Gramma been so glad to see her home. She leaned heavily against the lower porch railing for a moment resting for her final assault on the steps. Despite the evening's misadventures, and the gnawing realization Kate was truly lost, she managed a weak smile. Orville, who had patiently waited for her at various points along the path to offer what little encouragement he could, was perched above her on the porch railing.

"Almost there, Orville," she said softly.

With a terrific exertion she lifted one leg up to the first step and grasping the railing firmly with both hands, slowly inched her way, step by step, upward to the landing. Once there she leaned forward and with a great final effort pulled the screen door open. She waited a second, gathered her strength, then wrapping both hands on the doorknob, turned it with her last ounce of power, and heard it click open.

It swung in, she allowed herself the pleasure of falling to her knees on the narrow entry rug just inside the door. She wanted so much to close her eyes and sleep, but she reached deep into the reservoir of strength derived from being both bullied and calloused by a lifetime spent on the plains of South Dakota.

Gramma crawled forward on hands and knees onto the kitchen linoleum and into the light. She paused and craned her neck up at the clock. Could it possibly be quarter after two? She closed her eyes for a long moment, felt herself wobble, almost collapse to her elbows, somehow stayed up, then forced herself to move slowly again toward the living room where the telephone rested on a small table next to a pastel patterned formal sitting chair.

Still on her knees, she glanced at the piece of paper Beth had carefully placed next to the phone a few minutes before she and Dave had driven off. The words *Best Western* were neatly printed, and just below, the motel's phone number. Running on empty now, Susan Flannery, South Dakota woman, sobbed uncontrollably as she tapped in the numbers.

With Gramma safely at home, Orville's escort mission was now complete. He steeled himself against strangling fatigue and throbbing, debilitating pain and scrambled north into the salted night sky.

Chapter Twenty-two
Time Waits for No Kid

THE PHONE RANG JUST AS COLE BORDERS WAS zipping up his fly. He was normally a meticulously clean man, but in this instance, he neglected to wash his hands. He did, however, quickly wipe them on his sharply creased khaki pants. Hurrying down the short hall to the desk, he picked up on the third ring.

"Ziebach County sheriff's office," he barked. "Deputy Borders."

The voice on the other end seemed distant and was shrouded in fuzzy background noise. "Hi, Cole. Dave Flannery here. I need some help."

Borders sat down in the big wooden chair behind the desk. He was a short, stocky man with the easy grace of an athlete. Glancing at his wrist watch, he leaned forward, pushed a stained coffee cup aside with the back of his big hand, picked up a pen, and jotted *02:34* on a yellow legal pad. Beside it he printed *Flannery*.

"What can I do for you, Dave? I'm alone in the office at the moment, but I'll do what I can." He leaned back in the round-backed wooden chair and wrapped his left hand around the back of his neck and squeezed, as if to force concentration to his brain.

"Listen, Cole, my wife Beth and I are just now getting up on the freeway at Rapid City headed west toward Sturgis on I-90. My mother called a couple of minutes ago from the ranch. Our daughter Kate has somehow gone missing."

"Dave, you mean missing from the house or what?" He wrote *Kate Flannery,* and the word *missing* on the pad.

"Yeah. She went fishing yesterday over at the river. She was supposed to be back home by five for dinner but never showed up. Mom waited until almost six, and then drove my truck out to search for her, but the truck got stuck in the river somehow, and there was no sign of Kate. Beth and I went to Rapid City yesterday to have us a look-see at a bull, but we're headed back home now."

Just then the police scanner squawked and a female voice filled the small office. "Are you there, Cole?"

"Hang on just a second, Dave, I've got a call on the scanner." He flipped a switch and said, "Ten–four. Evening, Gladys. Whatcha need?"

"We got us a bad roll-over on two twelve about a mile west of Lantry. Can you send someone to help?"

"Injuries?" Cole asked. He picked up his coffee cup and drained it.

"First report says one fatality, and three others with undetermined injuries. Teenagers, beer, and speed, sounds like."

"I'm tied up here, Gladys. We've got a missing girl call just now coming in and I'm alone in the office. Travis is on a call down at Red Scaffold, but he should be freed up shortly. I'll send him your way quick as I can."

"Ten–four, Cole. 'Preciate it."

The deputy flipped the switch. "Sorry for the interruption, Dave. There's an accident over by Lantry and the call just came in. They need us to lend a hand." He paused. "I take it Kate went fishing alone?" He added the words *fishing in the river* beside Kate's name on the pad.

"Well, not exactly. She's got a wild hawk with her. The hawk came back to the ranch without Kate though."

"Did you say hawk?"

"Yeah. It's a long story, Cole. I'll explain later."

"How old is Kate now?"

"She'll be thirteen in a couple of weeks, middle of September. She's a good kid. Not the kind to run off. Never gives us any trouble at all."

"Tell you what. I'm gonna call Ben at home, and we'll get the two other guys in here as soon as possible. I imagine the first thing we'll do is head out to the river. Where does she usually fish? He wrote the number *13* and the word *hawk*.

"Do you remember where my dad caught you and me drinking beer when we were in high school?"

"Sure do," Cole said. "Your dad took the keys to your truck and we had to walk back to the ranch. She fishes out there, huh? Dahl's Bend, isn't it?" He wrote the words *Dahl's Bend* on the pad.

"Yep. Same exact place. We've been going out there to fish since she was five years old. The last year or two we've let her go alone because there isn't a thing out there to hurt her, and she's an excellent swimmer. I'm almost positive she's not in the…" Dave's voice broke off.

"Okay, Dave. We'll get started searching for her as soon as the guys get in here. Still three hours or so until sun's up, but we've got Charlie's dog and lots of lights so we'll get us a start on the search."

"Thanks, Cole. Beth and I will meet you out there at the river as soon as we can. I think we can be there in about three hours. If you go out to the house, Mom will give you something of Kate's for Charlie's dog to get a fix on. I'll call her and tell her you guys will be along. Okay?"

"Will do, Dave. Drive safely. See you out there then. Bye."

Cole sighed and thought, *How does a law enforcement officer tell one of his best friends not to drive like a crazy man when his daughter's life is at stake?* One hundred and sixty-five miles at night on South Dakota back roads in three hours? Deputy Borders's algebra wasn't going to get him into Cal Tech graduate school, but it was sufficient to calculate $v = d/t$. He quickly jotted some numbers down on the pad. Frowned.

Averaging fifty-five for three hours at night on unlit country roads is next to crazy, he thought.

With Dave's, "Thanks, Cole, appreciate it," still ringing in his ear, Deputy Cole Borders punched in Sheriff Ben Dredge's home number from memory. Tapping the pad with his pen point, he waited patiently to hear his boss's voice.

Then he wrote the words, *possible drowning.* He flipped the page under, glanced at his watch, and quickly wrote: *02:44. Rollover help request. Lantry. Radio Travis.*

Chapter Twenty-three
Flushed

ORVILLE COASTED TO A PICTURE PERFECT, ONE-legged landing next to Kate's baseball cap. But, before he had even tucked his wings tight to his body, he pushed off and took to the air again. Hushed voices above him required investigation.

Once he reached altitude he discerned the silhouettes of two hawks flying in tandem formation over the river about half a mile north of him. He was certain he recognized the shapes, but was flabbergasted red-tails were flying in the dark. To say hawks never fly at night would be untrue, but the circumstances would have to be extreme to warrant such risky business.

Flying at top speed, Orville closed within seconds and was directly behind the pair without them being aware of his presence. "Klur," he warned loudly. *Identify yourselves!*

The pair split instantly—standard evasive protocol—the one in front climbing into a vertical spin and turning left, while the bulkier one dropped abruptly and banked hard right. Orville accelerated and followed the more aggressive flyer climbing into a *Catch Me If You Can* loop above him. Even as the chase quickened he admired the flyer's ability. He knew immediately this was a superbly trained flyer.

He closed the gap and certain now he recognized the shape, called out, "Did you by any chance graduate from Prairie Winds Flight School in 2009?"

Glancing over her shoulder, Annabelle instantly banked hard right and responded, "Orville?"

His beak stretched into a wide grin. "Annabelle? What in the world are you doing up here in the middle of the night? Have you gone bonkers?"

She slowed and touched wingtips with him. "Orville, how good to see you again. I think of you often."

"Same," he said, rather shyly. "Terrific climb just now. You were really booking. With whom are you flying?"

"Professor Higgins," she said. "We'd better locate him fast. He might be in grave danger flying alone in the dark."

"He's safely grounded on the riverbank right below us," Orville said. "Stay tight and follow me down."

As soon as Orville landed, Higgins noticed something terribly wrong with Orville's leg. Before he could speak though, Orville greeted his former teacher as he would any honored elder, bowing low and touching the side of his beak to the ground near Higgins's talons.

"Orville," he said, "It's good to see you once again. You've suffered an injury?"

"Professor Higgins, sir, just a scratch. How are you, sir?"

"On the ground I'm fine. Don't much like flying in the dark anymore. Touch of nyctophobia I guess. Don't see as well as I used to. Fortunately I had Annabelle's young eyes to guide me up there. What brings you out at such an hour?"

"There's a young girl, sir, a dear friend of mine. She's somehow fallen into a nearby well and needs my help. I took a tumble about a week ago and she's been nursing me back to health."

Annabelle's eyes widened and her beak fell open in surprise. She said, "The very reason we're out tonight. I heard what I thought was a cry for help as I was flying near here at dusk. It must be the girl you speak of. If she's fallen into a well, it's no wonder I noticed her cap on the ground but couldn't see her. She wears a Cubs baseball cap, right?"

"That's her," Orville said. "We've no time to waste. I fear greatly for her life."

Higgins fluffed his wings. "Lead the way, lad. Our clear duty is to help whenever we're called. Fly low and keep the pace reasonable so I can follow."

"You go ahead, Orville," Annabelle said. "I know you can see the obstacles so we'll stick like glue right behind you. Level off at sixty feet and I'll escort Professor Higgins. Keep the speed at twenty and we'll be safe enough."

Before Higgins could protest he lacked nothing but youthful eyes, and did not require coddling or an escort service, Orville was aloft. Higgins would have gladly paid a dear price for a quality pair of army night vision goggles. He made a mental note to purchase a pair at first opportunity.

Annabelle followed Orville up immediately, and Higgins pulled in less than a foot behind her in tight formation. In a matter of two or three pretty hairy minutes of blind flight they glided to a gentle landing beside Kate's cap. Higgins had often imagined the extreme stress pioneering pilots must have felt flying through fog or stormy weather before radar was invented. Flying blind, he knew, was no picnic.

"Watch your step," Orville said. "There was a cover over this well at one time, but it's long gone rotten. Kate must have stepped on it and fallen through."

Higgins didn't care to ask the difficult question, and thankfully Annabelle saved him from it. "Are you sure she's still alive?" she whispered.

"Not sure, at all," Orville replied with a brusque tone his two companions had never heard from him before. "But I aim to find out. We're best friends."

He gazed long at Annabelle with a profound tenderness seldom seen in a hawk's eyes. He reached out and touched wingtips with her, and then with Higgins. Before either could say, "Be careful," Orville disappeared into the black hole.

The average Sears Roebuck & Company shovel is fifty-eight inches long. Unlike early gravediggers who approximated the width and length of the average casket as their hole pattern, pioneer well diggers often used the shovel's length as the diameter measurement of the circular hole they labored upon.

Since the average male red-tail's wingspan is from forty-six to forty-eight inches, Higgins realized instantly Orville would have great difficulty in extending his wings wide enough to catch air. Even if he was able to fly in the exact center of the cylinder, certainly no easy task, he would have, at most, a mere four or five inches clearance on each side. Even a tiny miscalculation by Orville could result in disaster.

At flight school, off the drop tower converted from a long abandoned grain silo, the students had sometimes practiced a desperation maneuver referred to as *The Flush*. With one wing fully extended and high, the opposite wing would be opened one fourth of the span and lowered. The result is a corkscrewing effect much like the swirling water when a toilet is emptied.

Higgins had cautioned his students *The Flush* was to be used sparingly in the direst of circumstances, and was risky to the extreme. But his young hawks—especially the dare-devil males who used it to show off for their admiring female classmates—thought it was ever so much fun twisting recklessly through the air. They, of course, were landing softly on a pile of old mattresses.

Higgins had been told recently after his retirement, due to parental pressure, *The Flush* maneuver had been banned from the school curriculum. He certainly understood the parents' concern, but he also knew this world was not built on timidity. In his mind it was just one more example of overzealous helicopter parenting interfering with the teacher's challenge of teaching critical flight procedures.

As Annabelle tottered over to the edge of the hole and peered in, she caught a quick glimpse of Orville spinning wildly down.

"Oh, Higgins, sir!" she cried. "He's flushed it!"

Higgins couldn't see a thing three feet past his beak so he quickly tilted his head, and silently counted—one thousand one—and waited for sounds of the expected crash. Instead he heard, far below, a soft splash. It is doubtful Orville had practiced *The Flush* more than five or six times total, yet he had just pulled off a near perfect one in complete darkness. Higgins's old heart swelled with pride, never mind he hadn't had much to do with it. More credit to Orville's courage than anything.

"Kate's unconscious, but breathing," Orville called up the deep shaft. His voice carried the eerie echo of the horrible place. "Her pack is waterlogged but still fairly buoyant. She's propped her head safely upon it. A pretty piece of good thinking."

"I'm going down to help Orville, Higgins, sir," Annabelle said. And in an eye-blink, before the teacher could find his voice to argue, and proving her mettle once more, Annabelle too was gone.

Just as her talons cleared the opening Higgins saw her left wing move to *The Flush* position and then she vanished from sight.

"Drat the darkness," Higgins muttered. He couldn't see a thing.

The bravery these two former students of his had demonstrated was mind-boggling. To dive into a narrow container of unknown depth contradicts even the most skilled flyer's logic and training. To execute it in total darkness is tantamount to suicide.

Unfortunately Annabelle's landing was harsher, and Higgins heard her utter a sharp cry of pain. Cupping a wing tip to his ear, he heard her mumble, through clenched beak, "I caught a talon in the wall, Orville. I think my leg snapped. Will I drown?"

"Of course not. Hold on to me," he replied, offering reassurance. At this point Orville had precious little else to offer. He gently cupped his wing around her body and pulled her close. "There, I've got you. There's a wonderful vet nearby to see to your injury. Not to worry."

"Are you okay?" Higgins called down. He reached for his under-wing double pouch leather holster he'd bought a few years back at the state fair in Huron. Just this morning he'd spent a pleasant hour carefully rubbing neat's-foot oil into it as a preservative and softener. His cell phone was in place as usual, but now he realized in his haste to meet Annabelle he had neglected to replace the ready store of M&M's in the second pouch when he had gone out the door.

"What has happened to my mind these days?" he said. "Double drat!"

"Annabelle's scuffed up a bit, Higgins, sir, but once I've checked Kate for injuries and I'm certain she is safely stabilized, I'll bring Annabelle up. She's okay for the moment."

Orville spoke with measured confidence, but Higgins knew there was virtually no way for him to launch himself vertically out of water with enough force to lift Annabelle's weight and his own. Even a bird like a Canada goose, designed specifically by nature to launch from water with a body vaguely resembling a World War II transport plane, requires a very long runway to get airborne.

For Orville, who would need to thrust with great vertical force with his powerful young legs off solid ground, it would be more than very difficult. Out of water, especially with Annabelle somehow clinging to his back, nigh impossible. Higgins couldn't imagine any red-tailed hawk strong enough for such a physically demanding stunt.

It was then Higgins remembered seeing the blood-crusted cast on Orville's leg. Just a scratch, indeed! It made him wonder too about Annabelle's condition. *More than likely,* he thought, *Annabelle has suffered a grievous injury, but Orville, not wanting to worry me unduly, has, no doubt, minimized it.*

It dawned on Higgins as he peered helplessly into the watery tomb, if these three were going to make it out alive, he must heed the call to action and be more than just a helpless onlooker.

There was just enough starlight for him to make out the number pad on his cell phone. He held it an inch or two from his eyes and using his beak quickly punched in the emergency number for the Prairie Winds School of Flight. Higgins knew at this late hour a computer at the school would automatically switch the call to the district superintendent's home phone. He cringed as it rang five long times before he finally heard a groggy, "Hello."

"Dr. Richfield? This is Boyd Higgins. Terribly sorry to bother you, Spud, but Orville Hampstead, Annabelle Matthews, and I are caught up in a very serious rescue operation out at the river quite near to Dahl's Bend."

Higgins heard a deep sigh, then, the words he knew were sure to come, "How can I help, Boyd?"

Higgins pictured the distinguished Dr. Richfield, his face feathers turning increasingly gray as the years rolled on, throwing back the covers and fumbling in the dark on a bedside table for his wing watch—then frowning at the awful hour. Spud Richfield and Higgins had flown countless sorties together up at the academy years ago, and Higgins held the utmost respect for him. Very few hawks, if any, could match Richfield's skill or courage aloft, and his reputation as an innovative and skilled school administrator was unparalleled.

"There's a young girl trapped in a well. She's been there for quite some time and may have suffered severe injuries in her fall. At the moment she is alive but unresponsive. Orville and Annabelle have flushed themselves down to her, but I'm afraid Annabelle has been injured too." He paused to let the words sink in.

"We need powerful help fast, and lots of it," Higgins continued, "to hoist the girl and Annabelle out. Currently, Orville is fine and monitoring the situation from below. I'm topside, at ground level, doing what I can."

Higgins stayed his beak, confident Dr. Richfield could quickly assess the situation, and with his years of experience, fabricate a rescue plan for a timely and safe remedy.

The sleep in Richfield's voice vanished, and he became fully articulate, retaining just a touch of his Texas birthplace twang.

"Young girl, you say? Must weigh under a hundred pounds then, could be as little as seventy-five. That's deadweight though, Boyd. It'll take our entire senior class in a *Power Climb* to lift her. How deep do you figure the well is?"

"Too dark to know for sure, but I estimated Orville fell for a fraction more than a second. He dropped, as I mentioned, using The Flush maneuver, not the usual Cannonball Drop. If I remember the manual correctly, Spud, it's thirty-five point five feet per second for a flush and fifty-two feet per second for the cannonball. I'm almost positive the well is forty feet, give or take. I was able to just barely count out a full second before I heard him hit the water."

"Those numbers sound about right, Boyd. My manual is on my desk at school so we'll have to rely on our combined memory. Forty-five feet of rope ought to be sufficient, but we'll bring sixty-five just to be on the safe side. Orville will require an extra three or four feet of line to fashion a support sling under the girl's arms, and we'll need fifteen feet of grip line above the well. Is the lad good with knots?"

Higgins felt his beak involuntarily open in a wide smile. "None better," he replied. "I have every confidence in Orville's ability. Flyer of the Year in 2009 you know."

Higgins heard the scratchy sound of bare talons moving across the floor and Richfield's wife Trudy's muffled voice, sounding a trifle irritated, in the background. Higgins was certain Dr. Richfield was peering out the window, assessing the flying conditions, and formulating a viable rescue plan.

"It's still too dark for truly safe flight, but the students' eyes are far better than mine. No doubt a few parents will grumble, but we'll have to chance it, no matter the risk. I'm going to sound the rescue alarm immediately. Where exactly are you?"

Higgins quickly gave him the compass coordinates, and Richfield replied, "We'll be there in no more than twenty minutes. Hang in there, Boyd."

The line went dead before Higgins could reply with the familiar red-tail prayer, "Deikrrt-Deimerrt-Deisoorrt." *God grant speed. God grant courage. God grant vision.*

Invigorated by Spud's can-do attitude, Higgins threw himself into the rescue operation with renewed enthusiasm. He quickly relayed the information concerning Dr. Richfield's plan down to Orville and Annabelle in hopes of buoying their spirits.

Using his talons as a makeshift rake, and cautious not to rain debris down on his comrades at the bottom of the hole, he hastily cleared decades of accumulated rubble off the remains of the decaying planks still partially covering the well. He took extreme care not to stumble and fall through, inadvertently becoming the well's fourth victim.

It was then Higgins heard the deep rumble of approaching vehicles. Almost directly south and slightly to the east, about two miles away, he could make out four headlights bumping slowly along through the night's dark curtain.

Chapter Twenty-four
Amazing Grace

INSIDE THE LEAD SUV, ZIEBACH COUNTY SHERIFF Ben Dredge peered into the night over the steering wheel. He was a big-shouldered, clean-shaven man with a full head of prematurely gray hair.

Next to him deputy Charlie Andrews sat quietly, hunched against the window. Charlie was tall and thin, perhaps six foot four and one hundred eighty pounds with a surprisingly deep and powerful voice. His nose was underlined with a full, dark brown moustache, and a khaki-colored sheriff's baseball cap covered what little hair remained on his head. Grace, a sleek, four-year-old black lab, tongue lolling, rode watchfully on the back seat.

They had made a quick stop at the Flannery ranch house a few minutes earlier. When Charlie opened the screen door and knocked, Gramma had come out on the porch in her robe and slippers clutching a brown paper grocery bag. In the time it had taken for her son Dave to alert the sheriff's department, and for them to respond, Gramma had gathered her strength by taking a hot shower and gulping down a cup of steaming tea. She was composed now, and confident these stalwart young South Dakota men would soon locate her granddaughter.

"Kate wore these pajamas last night," she said, handing the bag to Charlie. "I do hope it helps." She gripped her robe at the throat with a bony fist. A taut, but hopeful smile tugged at her lips.

"We'll find her, ma'am," Ben said with conviction. "It's real easy to get turned around out there and start walking the wrong direction. Happens all the time." He patted her shoulder reassuringly and stepped down off the porch to the bottom step. Turning back to face her, he said, "Don't you worry now, Mrs. Flannery, a kid her age can survive a night outside easy as pie. Cold and hungry is how it usually works out."

Ben rested his hand on the emergency brake, the engine idling smoothly, before starting up the long Flannery driveway. He calculated out loud.

"Daughter Kate was supposed to be home by five. It's coming up on four-thirty now. She's been wherever she is for almost twelve hours. Assuming she stopped walking about ten o'clock when it would be too dark to see much, she could be anywhere from five to a dozen miles from here."

"Only east or west though," Charlie said.

"How do you figure?" Ben asked. He released the brake and slowly navigated around the flowerbeds. Craning his neck, he stole a quick glance back at the porch to make sure Gramma was safely inside the house.

"Well, when she was done fishing and ready to head home, the river would be to her north, and it's not likely she waded across it trying to get home. So cross north off. If she had walked south, like she should have, she would have come to her family's property and seen the house. Apparently didn't happen, so cross south off too. Must've gone east toward New York City or west toward Seattle."

Charlie glanced back over his left shoulder into the back seat at the lab. "What do you think, Grace?" he said. "Did Kate walk toward the Big Apple or the Big Puddle?"

Grateful to be included in the conversation Grace replied by leaning eagerly forward between the seats, but didn't say anything.

"Don't you slobber on me now, Deputy Grace. This is a fresh uniform," Charlie said with a laugh.

Ben, keeping his left hand on the steering wheel, managed a quick scratch on Grace's forehead. "You think maybe the girl's in the river?" he asked. It was not something he cared to think about, but it was his business to conjecture.

Charlie sighed. There was a long silence as both men and Deputy Grace considered what might be.

"Possible, I guess," said Charlie, "but my boy Chris took swimming lessons with her out at the pool back in June, and he talked about how good a swimmer she is. I think he's kind of sweet on her, to tell you the truth. Time she grows up, Kate'll be a real beauty just like her mom. Anyway, Chris said Kate could out-swim all the girls and most of the boys. You remember Max Harney's kid? Pete, I think his name is. Big star on the football and basketball team last year? Chris said Kate beat Harney in the crawl and backstroke. A kid can swim like a dolphin ain't gonna drown easy."

The car was quiet for a moment as they slowed, then bumped across the main road by the Flannery mailbox and headed toward the river.

Charlie added, "That river ain't got no fight in it this time of year. Hard to believe a kid who's such a good swimmer could drown in it, 'less she hit her head on a rock or something."

"I'm thinking the same thing," Ben said. He glanced at his rearview mirror and caught a flash of headlights. "Here comes Old King Cole behind us. Nice of Terri to come in early for her shift so he could leave the office and help us search for the girl."

Off to the right the eastern sky was beginning to lighten, as if someone was slowly prying the lid off a big old hatbox filled to the brim with bubbling volcanic liquid fire. At the bottom edge of the lid there was just a hint of purple, as the black of night began its first romance of the day with the dawdling sun. The air was still and cool, ready to greet another perfect morning on the plains.

"Be light soon," Charlie said. "Where we gonna start?"

"Well," Ben replied, "I guess we'll take us a quick gander down at the river where she was fishing. See if we can see anything there. If she's in the river we won't be able to see much 'til light's up, and she could have floated ten miles downstream by now I suppose. Just don't think she's in the river somehow."

The butte loomed, a dark, two-layer chocolate cake shape off to their left now. Both men glanced over at it.

"Cole, Dave, and I walked right over the top of that danged hill about twenty-five years ago," Ben said. "Dave's dad caught us drinking beer out there at the river and made us walk back to the house. Boy was Dave's old man mad. Never seen a man crazy mad before. Name was Ernie if I remember right."

Charlie nodded.

"I doubt Dave's had a beer since," said Ben. "Time we got back to Dave's house his dad had called Cole's parents, mine too, and the baseball coach. We were juniors, and Cole was the best shortstop in the league. Dave was the starting catcher, and I pitched every other game. The next afternoon we went out to practice same as always, but right after batting practice, coach set the whole team down in the bleachers. Coach has this painful look on his face. He says, 'Any you boys drink some beer out at the river yesterday?'"

Ben chuckled. "It's funny now, but it sure wasn't funny then. Dave knew his dad had called the coach so he raised his hand and said, 'Coach, I had a couple beers out there while I was fishing for catfish.' Big lie right there. We didn't even have our fishing gear with us. If I remember right all we had was a half case of cold Miller beer. Coach says, 'Dave, you're a real good catcher, but rules are rules. We'll see you out here again next year. You're done for this season. Take it to the locker room, son.'

"So, Dave stands up, grabs his catcher's mitt, and starts walking away. About then coach says, 'Anybody else?' So I raise my hand. Coach says, 'Ben Dredge, your dad was one of the best pitchers this county has ever seen. Nobody even close to him in raw talent, 'cept for you.

Rules are rules. I hope you'll be turning out again next spring.'

"A few minutes later Cole was walking along behind Dave and me. His season was over too."

Charlie laughed. "Coach Phillips was something else. Darn good social studies teacher too. Loved history. Heard he had a stroke recently."

The two SUVs stopped side by side at the river's edge. The three men climbed out and gathered at the spot where Orville had taken Kate's fishing pole from her before his flight back to the ranch.

"Dave's truck ain't much of a boat is it?" Cole said. The truck was still parked, a black looming barge plowing against the current near the center of the river. The headlights, off now, stared forlornly upstream.

"If this weren't so serious it'd be pretty funny," Ben said quietly. He flipped on a long black flashlight and swept the near bank with the bright beam.

"A pile of clothes or something over there," Charlie said, pointing with a long arm. A dark frown skittered across his face, making his mustache turn down at the corners. "Let's take a gander."

The three men followed the flashlight's beam down to the river's edge. Charlie kneeled and without touching it studied the clothing carefully. "It's a wet dress and one of those slip things. I'll bet when Gramma Flannery got out of the truck she got soaked and took them off here. Musta walked home naked."

Despite the situation all three men laughed at the thought of a seventy-eight-year-old woman hiking the three miles back to the ranch in her birthday suit.

The laughter seemed out of place, but it relieved and smoothed over the grinding, unspeakable gut fear all three men had felt when the clothing was first spotted. They had been in attendance at rape and murder scenes before—the very worst part of their business.

"Charlie, why don't you get Grace out and give her a good whiff of Kate's pajamas? Let's find out which way Grace thinks she started walking."

In a flash Grace was out of the sheriff's vehicle and on leash. Being careful not to touch the contents, Charlie tore the paper bag down on the corners and pulled the flaps down flat to the ground. Grace quickly buried her nose in the garment. Almost instantly her brain registered the distinct odor of a particular human being among a possible six and a half billion other human beings on earth. Satisfied she had all the information she needed to do her job, she strained toward the water's edge.

Charlie unsnapped the taut leash and followed obediently while the two other law enforcement officers watched intently from the bank.

Nose to the ground, Grace went first to the water's edge, paused, then waded in up to her belly. Just short of midstream she stopped, held her head high, nose quivering, nostrils wide, sifting the air for clues. Dipping her head, she lapped eagerly at the cold water, drinking deeply. Her thirst quenched, she turned and walked back to dry ground and gave herself a good shake. Then she followed her nose up to where Orville and Kate had eaten their lunch together. She paid particular attention to the spot where Kate had laid on her back reading *The Hobbit* to Orville.

"She and the hawk must have been over there," Cole called. "Grace seems pretty sure of the spot."

"What hawk?" Ben asked. The three men now surrounded the rock-lined fire pit.

"When Dave called from Rapid City he said Kate had gone fishing with a hawk. Sounded kind of weird to me, but he said he'd tell me about it later."

The eastern sky was gray now with just a tinge of orange as the hatbox lid continued to tilt slowly open.

Ben said, "Don't think she's in the river. The current is so slow it wouldn't hurt a Ford truck, much less a Flannery kid. I'll bet whatever happened to her happened between here and the ranch house. We just now drove the trail and she wasn't anywhere along there or we'd have seen her." He paused, his mind following the same twisting strands of logic Orville's reasoning had earlier. "Makes me think she either walked directly over that butte or west of it. What do you guys think?" He switched off the flashlight.

"You're probably right," Cole answered. "The old Dahl homestead is on the other side of the butte, a bit to the west. Ain't much left of it, just a jumble, but maybe she was poking around there and hurt herself. You know how kids are. Even if there ain't no way to get hurt, they'll find one. Could have stepped on an old nail or something. Cut herself on some broken glass maybe."

"What do you think, Charlie?" Ben asked.

"Doubt if she's in the river. If she is, we're way too late to do anything about it anyway. Why don't Grace and I snoop around there by where the path comes down to the riverbank? Kate probably started out for home somewhere up in there. You and Cole can follow us in one of the vehicles."

"You gonna let her run off leash?" Ben asked.

"Not yet. Still too dark. If she's got a good fix she'll pull me along. If she acts like she's lost the scent, I'll let her go 'til she picks it up again. The butte's just a mile or so from here, so we can hook up again there."

While the two officers climbed back into Ben's rig, Charlie got down on his knees next to the paper bag holding Kate's pajamas. He snapped the leash back on her collar.

"Grace," he said gently, pulling the dog close with a long arm, feeling her trembling strength and warmth, "there's a little girl lost out here somewhere. Will you find her for us?"

Grace's ears caught the sound first and she tilted her quivering black nose up, as if to catch a scent. Six hundred and fifty feet directly overhead, the soft whirr of thirty-two pairs of beating wings flying in tandem, rent the air.

Charlie, still on his knees, lifted his eyes toward the fading stars. "What do you hear, Deputy Grace?" he murmured. "Angels' wings?" He stared long and hard at the night sky like an ancient ship's navigator, as if seeking directional guidance from above. Receiving none, he turned back to his business.

Carefully he slid his hand under the sack, picked up Kate's nightclothes and held them again to Grace's nose. No need. Amazingly, Kate's existence was already locked in.

Chapter Twenty-five
Monumental Effort

IGGINS WASN'T SURPRISED THE SHERIFF'S VEHIcles drove right by him on their way to the river. It was still almost perfectly dark and even if it were light, they most likely wouldn't have noticed an old hawk poking around in the dirt a quarter mile away. But he was sure surprised a few minutes later when a boiled spaghetti strand of thirty redtailed scholars, their vivacious teacher, Ms. Chawla Ride, and district superintendent, Spud Richfield, came pouring out of the inky sky almost on top of him.

Spud quickly introduced Higgins to Chawla, a superb flier who had first come to South Dakota from India as an exchange student. She had finished first in her class at the academy, the first female to earn such a distinction, and then joined the staff at Prairie Winds as a replacement after Higgins had retired.

In many ways her career path was much the same as Higgins, except he had been born and raised near Kadoka, South Dakota. Since she had taken over his former teaching duties, he had heard many positive comments about her. Even in the dim light he could see her feathers were slightly darker than his and he detected a hint of a delightful British accent in her voice. To Higgins's eye, she was quite attractive, even without makeup or the gold wing bangles he'd heard she favored.

The students gathered around Higgins in a semicircle while he quickly explained the situation. Chawla, annoyed by a bit of excited whispering while he spoke, silenced them with a meaningful frown and a sharp flip of her silver-tipped wing. Higgins's heart soared to see such high expectations and firm discipline from such a young teacher.

Dr. Richfield carefully skirted the well, walking slowly around the perimeter. "First things first," he said. "Ms. Ride, I need your four strongest fliers."

"Doug, Roland, Phil, Dale," she called without the slightest hesitation. "Front and center. Pronto!"

Higgins smiled as the four powerfully built young hawks hurried to obey their teacher.

"These planks need to be moved to the side out of our way," Richfield instructed. "Two of you on each end. Lift with your legs lads. Spare your backs. No time to waste."

Richfield turned to the rest of the assembly just off to one side. "As soon as the opening is cleared we'll drop the line down to Orville. Once he ties off a loop under the girl's arms, each of you will elevate, snatch the rope, grip talons and grab beaks, just as you do in the rescue drill off the flight tower at school. Assuming the girl weighs less than one hundred pounds, I've calculated each of you will have to lift at least two and a half pounds of the girl's weight, plus of course, your own. I'm told some ants can lift from ten to twenty times their own weight, so we should be able to lift at least twice our own weight to a height of forty feet off the ground. It won't be easy, but as my mom was wont to say, 'RT Spud Richfield, few things in this world worth doing are easy. So just flex your wings and get to it!'"

His magnificent wings fluttered open for a moment, as if illustrating the message his mother had drilled into him when he was a wee fledgling.

The students giggled when they heard his easy use of his first name, Spud. They of course addressed him as Dr. Richfield at school, and prior to this moment probably had no inkling of what his first name even was. It was merely his way of breaking the tension all were feeling.

"I want the four hulks"—the class giggled again as he gestured with a wing tip at the four students moving planks—"at the top end of the rope; they will pull it taut and hover directly over the well's opening. At your teacher's command the rest of you, one at a time in your teacher's designated order, will fly up and grab a tight grip on the rope a few inches below the tail of the student just above you."

Richfield glanced slowly around the group, making momentary eye contact with each student. "Once all thirty of you have taken a strong purchase with your talons, Ms. Ride and I will join you on the rope, and then, at the precise moment when all sixty-four wings beat as one, honorable retiree, Professor Higgins will give us the order to fly. At his command, and this is crucial, we all, in perfect unison, must give fifty of our very strongest, short interval wing beats to drag the girl out of the water.

"As you well know from your studies, the water will create a tremendous drag on her body and it will take every ounce of our combined strength to extricate her from it. Once she's clear of the water, things should get easier for us. I'm asking Higgins to sing out the fifty beats. On the fifty-first beat, we all must put the pedal to the metal and give it all we've got with longer wing beats."

Even Chawla Ride chuckled at the old-fashioned expression as the students laughed loudly. Higgins couldn't help but join in, despite his misgivings about what they were attempting to accomplish.

There were several unknowns gnawing away at him: What if Kate weighed more than one hundred pounds? Had Dr. Richfield included the weight of the rope in his calculations? Surely it must weigh at least ten pounds. Would all of the students be up to the tremendous task of performing fifty, backbreaking, short interval beats? If one failed, could the others bear the extra burden? These unknown factors made Higgins uneasy, but not wanting to question the superintendent in front of the students he respectfully kept his silence.

As soon as it was quiet again Richfield continued: "We will ascend vertically in an Up the Elevator Shaft power climb until we hear Higgins cue us the girl is safely out of the well. Once we hear his call we will fly exactly ten meters north toward the river and slowly reduce our wing force to gently lower the rope until the girl is lying safely on the ground. Higgins will again notify us, and all but the four topmost fliers, the hulks, will let go of the rope and return to ground. Any questions?"

Dr. Richfield, like any good educator, allowed plenty of time for the students to voice concern or ask for clarification. With none forthcoming, he smiled.

"Good," he said. The affection and trust he felt for them was sincerely displayed in his eyes.

Higgins too was proud of these young ones. Even now he could tell they were the equals of his best classes of years ago. Their eyes absolutely glittered with their willingness—even eagerness to tackle what would surely amount to a monumental effort.

Nodding his noble graying head toward Ms. Ride, Dr. Richfield said, "Lend a beak, Chawla."

The pair of educators quickly grabbed one end of the rope and snaked it over to the edge of the now yawning hole. It was the yellow-braided type of line favored by water skiers, and there was no doubt about its ability to hold the girl's weight.

Digging his talons in, Higgins leaned over the edge and called out, "Orville, we're sending the rope down. Secure it under Kate's armpits and we'll attempt to haul her out."

The instant the word attempt had escaped Higgins's beak he regretted it, as it sounded to his own ears, and most likely to the students as well, he was not fully convinced Richfield's plan would work. He certainly didn't intend to plant any seeds of doubt in their minds, and yet he had just done so.

How true it is, he thought, *carelessly spoken words are like regretful arrows speeding from the bow—unable to be called back—no matter how poisonous they might be. Too late! Too late! Drat!*

"Will do," Orville replied. His confident words spiraled back up the shaft toward Higgins.

Meanwhile Ms. Ride organized her students in a tight line adjacent to the well's opening. They stood quietly like brave, little feathered soldiers awaiting their signal to jump into the fray.

Two minutes later Orville's voice boomed upwards again. "All secure! Hoist away when ready."

Dr. Richfield directed the four hulks to the far end of the rope and, with Doug bravely leading the way, they gripped the rope firmly in their talons. At Richfield's firm command, they were airborne.

About fifteen feet directly over the well they hovered, drawing the rope taut. Immediately Ms. Ride tapped the first student on the back with her wingtip. One by one, cued by their teacher, the students rose swiftly, caught the rope, secured their own grip, and added their relaxed wing beats to the team effort. In a moment all thirty students were attached to the rope, fluttering like feathery ribbons on a windy kite tail, and then Chawla Ride and Spud Richfield were also airborne, gripped and ready directly below the students.

Higgins waited a moment until all wings were beating in perfect synchronization, then without further hesitation he shouted, "Kleeett," at the top of his lungs. *Fly like never before!*

Instantly the air above the well swelled with terrific, agitated currents rolling off straining young wings as the rope started to creep ever so slowly upward, inch by inch. In less than a minute Higgins had crisply counted out the fiftieth quick stroke. The fliers made a smooth transition into the longer, more efficient stroke of the Up the Elevator Shaft power climb, but still the rope barely inched upward.

Higgins stood helplessly at the edge, peering upward and listening to the sounds of tremendous force being applied. His steady count, much like an urging coxswain counting rhythmic cadence in a boat of eight college oarsmen, kept the young hawks straining against their growing fatigue. He was certain these young wings had never trained for such a sustained power climb and would soon be exhausted. The rope had moved upward no more than two or three hard-earned feet, and Kate's lower body, from the knees down, still dangled in the water.

Above the well now were agonizing grunts and groans as the brave fliers sucked up their last desperate reserves of strength. For a few thrilling seconds the rope moved upward at a quicker pace as Kate's body escaped the water and was pulled perhaps ten feet above the surface, but a moment later the battle was lost. The weight was simply too much for such young wings and hearts. The movement upwards had come to a sudden standstill and the flyers, gasping for air and groaning with pain, strained just to keep gravity from sucking them all down into the well.

Dr. Richfield quickly realized the plan had failed. He shouted out, "Reduce power!"

Slowly the ghastly black hole swallowed the straining line and then went slack as Kate's weight below became buoyant in the water once more.

Ms. Ride prudently left her place on the rope and, hovering next to her desperately tired students, ordered them down. Soon all thirty of them, even the four hulks, huffing and puffing, collapsed on the ground, utterly exhausted.

The mute morning sky above, now dusty gray like a barren slate floor in a medieval castle courtyard, bore silent witness to the failure. Chawla Ride and Spud Richfield stumbled about on unsteady legs among the students, giving tender wingtip pats of appreciation and offering gentle words of encouragement for the students' backbreaking though futile efforts.

The students had willingly given their all, and though surely disappointed at their failure to rescue Kate, Higgins was certain they would remember this day as one of their finest moments.

Prominent at their school's entrance hangs a large polished brass plaque just above the door: *To Try—And To Succeed—Our Mission. To Try—And To Fail—Yet Honorable. Not Trying—Dishonorable.* Each morning as the students arrived at the school they would each touch the plaque with a wingtip as they came in the door. Today these students had surely lived up to their school's lofty yet honorable ideals.

Meanwhile Orville had carefully removed the rope from around Kate's armpits and placed her head safely back onto the floating backpack. His heart thudded with despair as he contemplated Kate's, Annabelle's, and perhaps even his own dreadful fate. He would never consider leaving until Kate and Annabelle were safely out of the hideous hole—or, forbid he even think it—perished.

The next step in reformulating a fresh rescue strategy became a moot point, because a big, black dog all slobbery and ferocious, charged down the slope of the butte toward the prone students.

Higgins, the first to spot the black intruder, shouted, "Trrreestt" *Snatch air!* Almost instantly most of the students, plus Ms. Ride and Dr. Richfield, scrambled safely aloft.

Momentarily frozen, mostly out of astonishment, Higgins did not react to his own call for safety. In mere seconds before the dog was upon him, a flash of red erupted out of the well. Orville, hearing Higgins's warning shout, and realizing the exhausted students could do little to protect themselves, had furiously launched himself like a rocket up and out of the dark cylinder.

When he cleared the opening and saw the hurtling dog, Orville braked, turned hard, and in a split second calculated his options. He accelerated and dove, then leveled off no more than a foot and a half off the ground. Higgins stared in awestruck wonder at Orville's near perfect, almost suicidal, Fire on the Wire attack straight at the thundering dog.

At the last instant, before a catastrophic head-on collision, Orville barrel-rolled over onto his back, and wings tucked, rocketed between the hairy, black phantom's legs like a hot grounder skipping under the glove of a wide-eyed shortstop. Orville pulled his legs tight to his body, extended the talons of his good leg, and plowed four shallow furrows in the dog's vulnerable underbelly.

Once Orville cleared the dog's tail, he climbed vertically in a tight corkscrew spin to perhaps one hundred feet, then looped, and dove hard, taking the stunned dog by surprise from above. This time Orville's talons raked the dog's back, leaving a fine spray of red droplets cascading to the ground.

The last glimpse of Orville was his body spinning rapidly like an Olympic skater fifteen feet above the well, as he re-flushed himself down to Kate and Annabelle. He alone could help them now.

Orville's breath-taking maneuvers certainly diverted the dog's attention, and at the very least, slowed its charge, buying crucial escape time for the slower students. It is certain Orville had seen the schematic for the Fire on the Wire maneuver in an Advanced Hawk Aerial Combat manual while browsing in the school library with his buddies during lunch hour. It is equally certain he had never actually performed one before, making his extraordinary actions all the more remarkable. Fire on the Wire is a highly sophisticated red-tail attack tactic seldom introduced before graduate school and utilized almost exclusively by the military.

The four hulks, who had been hurriedly gathering up the rope before making their escape, no doubt were saved by Orville's bravery. They just managed to elude the leaping dog's snapping jaws. In the aftermath a solitary, bloodstained tail feather fluttered to the ground. Close call, yes, but what a terrific story these young fliers would be able to relate to their nestlings and grand-nestlings someday.

Alas, the heroic students had carried off the rope, a potentially useful tool.

Chapter Twenty-six
Nose to Beak

DEFYING ALL REASONABLE LOGIC, LIKE AN ABSOlute idiot, Higgins stood his ground and faced his ferocious foe. He wasn't about to have a sixty-pound dog go tumbling down the well shaft on top of the girl and his two companions, nor was he keen to let the dog have a go at himself either.

Higgins fluffed himself up like a gravely insulted and indignant baseball umpire. He spread his wings and gave the dog six-bits worth of his best Malaysian cobra hiss. He hadn't had a serious confrontation for several years, but he knew from experience with several near-miss eagle clashes, and from dealing with thieving, conspiratorial crows, and a cunning coyote or two, most creatures will at least hesitate at the sight of a riled, red-tailed hawk. To protect his comrades and himself, he desperately needed to stall the dog's charge and buy a few seconds of time.

The dog, infuriated at Orville's searing talon wounds recently inflicted on her belly and back, and frustrated in her attempt at vengeance, garnering nothing but an empty bite of fleeing hawk butt, loosed her barbarous anger on Higgins. Nevertheless, Higgins stood, talons planted firmly, at the precipice of the well—and the sleek dog, powerful legs churning, bore down on him at close to twenty miles an hour—like a determined baseball player racing down the third base line trying to score the go-ahead run over, around, or through the catcher at home plate. It was a marvelous squeeze play!

Higgins closed his eyes and braced himself for the inevitable big time collision, when a shout of salvation thundered, "Grace! Freeze!"

The dog, responding instantly to her training, slammed on the brakes and slid over the top of Higgins, almost knocking them both into the well. They stood nose to beak, but as startled and terrified as Higgins was, he didn't budge an inch.

Up on the butte now Higgins could see a vehicle stop at the edge. In a flash, the uniformed man whose timely shout had prevented a catastrophe of the highest magnitude arrived. He ignored Higgins, and breathing heavily from his chase after Grace, snapped a stout, restraining leash on her collar. Almost immediately, two other smartly dressed officers loped down the hill toward the well.

"Whatcha got, Charlie?" the larger of the two yelled.

"There's a wild hawk, for one thing, and just before I got here about twenty-five more of 'em took off flying. They were carrying a rope or some string with 'em. Grace must have broken up their little tea party."

Higgins, grievously wounded by such a thoughtless remark, almost forced him to ask—"Officer Charlie, what other kind of hawk is there but a wild one? A zoo's strongest cage cannot even begin to harness a hawk's wildness. And furthermore, sir, your comment referring to what was nothing less than a magnificent rescue effort as a 'little tea party' is ludicrous at best."

But with Grace just inches away, staring Higgins down with frothy strings of slobber dripping off her tongue, he thought it best to keep quiet. He was absolutely certain nothing less than bloody revenge filled her agitated mind. Charlie's tight grip on Grace made Higgins feel a whole lot better.

"Big hole in the ground here too, Ben," Charlie added, as the other two men walked up. "Looks like an old well. Musta been that Norwegian geezer Dahl's when he still lived out here. I heard he died just after the war, 'bout 1946 or '47, so it's been abandoned for sixty some years. Never had no wife or kids I've heard of."

"Gramma Flannery said Kate was wearing a Cubs baseball cap when she left home yesterday," Ben said. "See it anywhere?"

Higgins had moved the cap out of the way a few yards to protect it while the four young hulks were removing the well cover. He opened a wing and pointed at the cap. His innocent gesture was a mistake, however, because Grace lathered herself up again, and Charlie had to take another turn around his wrist with the leather strap to keep her from getting a face full of red-tail talons. Even a doddering old hawk like Higgins will protect himself when things get too hairy.

"There's the cap," Officer Cole said. "Betcha anything Kate's in that well."

Anticipating their next move, Higgins fluttered aside, carefully keeping the well between Grace and himself while the three men gathered carefully at the edge of the opening. They leaned over and peered down. Ben snapped on his big flashlight and pointed it down the hole. "Kate Flannery," he called. "Are you okay?"

There was no answer. "It appears she's floating on an old life preserver or something, don't it, Ben?" Charlie said. "Kate!" he boomed.

Charlie's big voice filled the hole and boomeranged back out to where they were standing. It was clear from her lack of response she was unconscious. Officer Charlie has one of those powerhouse voices people joke about as being loud enough to wake the dead.

"There's a couple more hawks swimming around down there too," Officer Cole said. "Wonder what all these hawks are doing around here?" He gestured toward Higgins. "Do you think they make nests underground?"

Higgins about laughed out loud when he heard such an absurd comment, but Grace had her eyes fixed on him, and he had no desire to stir her up again. The officer's silly question went unanswered, because just then a white car came roaring into view, spitting dust in a big cloud behind it.

Ben waved the flashlight high over his head and said, "Here come the Flannerys."

Chapter Twenty-seven

Invention's Mother

EVEN BEFORE THE CAR CAME TO A COMPLETE stop, the passenger door flew open and a frantic woman dashed toward the officers. "Where's our girl?" Beth cried. "Where's Kate?"

The driver, a tall, serious-faced man, had braked the car to a sliding stop, flung his door open, and came running. "Have you got her, Ben?" he shouted. "Where is she?"

Sheriff Ben Dredge stepped toward the couple and held out his arms as if to embrace old friends. His voice was strong, but gentle. "She's down in this old well, Dave. Must have accidentally fallen in on her way back from fishing. We just got here two minutes ago ourselves."

"Is she alive?" Beth cried, trying to push past Ben.

Ben took one step back then held his ground, as if to say, *This is as far as I'm letting you go, folks.* He kept his arms wide like a security fence. "Beth, we put a light on her and her head is out of the water, but she doesn't respond to our call. We won't know how she is until we get down to her."

The other two officers, Charlie and Cole, had also stepped between the couple and the well as their training dictated, forming a human barricade to protect the Flannerys from potentially unbearable grief.

Dave Flannery spoke up, clearly upset. "What's your plan, Ben? Let's get on with it."

"Dave, the well appears to be somewhere between forty and fifty feet deep. We've got at best twenty feet of rope in our vehicles so we've got us a real problem."

"You've got an electric winch and cable on your rig," Dave said, pointing at the vehicle parked atop the butte. "We can use that. I'll ride the cable down and grab her."

Ben glanced down at the ground for an instant and then ran a rough-skinned hand sheepishly through his charcoal hair. "The county bought us three new Ford Explorers two years ago, Dave, but the council said there was only enough money for one electric winch. Travis is clear down to Lantry helping them with a rollover. He's driving the Ford with the winch. I'm fixing to get him on the radio, but he's a good hour and a half from here, at least."

Officer Ben Dredge and rancher Dave Flannery had been friends since first grade. They had played football, basketball, and baseball together. They had stood against the wall of the school gym together getting their courage up and arguing about which one of the pretty girls on the other side of the gym floor they should ask to dance. They had sat together red-faced, trying hard not to giggle, in the principal's office when some prank of theirs had been uncovered. When they were juniors in high school they had been kicked off the baseball team together. Ben had stood up for Dave and Beth as best man at their wedding fifteen years ago. Now they stood nose to nose, inches apart, one a stalwart defender of the law, the other, a frantic father.

"We don't have that kind of time, Ben. I've got plenty of rope in my truck down at the river," Dave said. His eyes were on fire and his voice rattled with impatience. "I've got all the tools we need to build a winch. What's left of Dahl's place over there should give us the wood we need for the supports and a spindle. You guys gather what you can, and I'll have Beth run me down to the river to get my truck."

"Your truck's been squatting in the river most of the night, Dave," Cole said. "She might not start up for you. Let me drive you down there just in case. If need be we can throw your tools and ropes in the Explorer."

A course of action had been decided without the need for official authority. The gold sheriff's badge on a chest became meaningless—they were all constructed of the same common fiber—South Dakota strong.

Dave wrapped a thick arm around his wife's shoulders and gently turned her back toward the car. "Hon," he said, "maybe it'd be best if you wait here. Use our cell and call Peterson Memorial in Philip and tell them we'll be bringing Kate in quick as we can. Better call Mom too and make sure she's okay."

Officer Cole was already jogging up the ridge to the butte where the Explorer was parked when Dave turned away from Beth and took off at a brisk trot after him.

Charlie pulled Grace over to one side and dropped the leash without unsnapping it. "Down," he ordered. Obediently, Grace dropped to her belly, but kept her dark eyes riveted on Higgins in a vengeful stare. Remembering it some nights keeps him awake, even now.

At this point though, Higgins was beginning to empathize with Grace. After all, he reasoned, she had merely been doing what she had been trained to do—track a lost child. Grace had no way of knowing the red-tails were a step ahead of the men in the rescue effort, and she had reacted instinctively to the hawks' presence at the site by charging them. After Orville strafed her belly and back, it was no wonder she was furious with Higgins. He made a mental note to apologize and explain it all to her later.

"I'll bet this pile of old boards covered the well at one time," Ben said. "When Kate walked by here it must've been too dark to see, and she fell in. Can't imagine why anybody would uncover an old well and just leave it open like a trap. Darn near criminal."

Of course Ben had no inkling four husky young hawks had just recently hoisted the well cover off after Kate had fallen through. Higgins realized with all the work still to do, now was not a good time to explain things, so he let it go.

"Give me a hand, Charlie. Let's move 'em out of the way." The two men easily tossed the boards farther aside in no time flat.

"You ever build a winch before?" Charlie asked.

Ben replied, "No, but how hard can it be? The homesteaders did it all the time. The first thing is to hustle over there and find six poles strong enough for two tripods, one on each side of the well. Know what I mean?"

Higgins kept silent and watched. He wanted to pitch in and help in the worst way, as is customary for all South Dakota red-tails, but these men were young, strong, and trained in rescuing people in trouble. He thought it prudent to just keep out of their way.

While the men were searching out boards, Higgins leaned over the edge of the well and explained to Orville what was happening up above. The gray skies had melted away now, replaced by diffuse blue shades laced with shafts of piercing gold. Enough light was cast for Higgins to clearly see the top of Kate's head floating above the surface of the water. It appeared Orville was supporting Annabelle to keep her out of the water; at what dear cost to himself, Higgins could but wonder.

"Sounds like a reasonable plan," Orville responded weakly. "Annabelle and I are okay so far, and Kate's airway is propped clear of the water." Despite his precarious situation and deteriorating strength, Orville's eyes glittered mischievously and a semblance of a grin crossed his face. "How're you and that big ol' dog making out?" he asked, as casually as if he and Higgins were perched side by side on a solid tree branch, chatting away a quiet afternoon. "I imagine I got her riled up some."

Higgins glanced over at Grace. "Let's put it this way—I've made her acquaintance. She did her job and you did yours."

The sun was rising fast on the eastern edge, and it was starting to warm up some. When Ben and Charlie returned they carried a big load of poles and a thick timber. They stacked it neatly beside the well. Then both men unzipped their jackets and dropped them to the ground.

Ten minutes later Dave's Ford pick-up came roaring around the side of the butte and parked next to the Toyota. In a flash Cole pulled the Explorer up beside him. Cars were piling up like the Rapid City mall parking lot on a busy Saturday afternoon.

Dave's pants were wet up to his waist where he'd waded out to climb into the truck. He jumped up in the truck bed as easy as a young kangaroo and started handing ropes and tools down to Cole who laid everything out nice and neat beside the well.

"We found some sturdy, eight-foot split fence railings on the other side of the house jumble," Ben said. "Old man Dahl must have kept a couple horses and a cow or two in a corral at one time. Maybe an ox to pull the plow."

"Those should be fine for the tripods," Dave said. Standing tall in the bed of his truck he added, "If you guys will lean three of those poles together I'll pound a couple of ten penny nails into 'em from up here."

He reached down, grabbed a steel claw hammer out of his toolbox and a fist full of nails from a brown paper bag. In a flash the nailing was done; Dave dropped the hammer in the dirt and cut a couple of short, three-foot lengths of rope with a big pocketknife he fished out of his jeans' pocket. Handing the rope pieces down to Charlie, Dave said, "Wrap these around the joints on top of those nails two or three times for extra strength."

In an eye-blink both tripods were firmly lashed together. Normally when hawks or men are building things they like to stand back from time to time to admire and congratulate themselves on the splendid progress they've made, but there was no gawking or easy men's chitchat going on here; no relaxed, cold beer swigging or hot coffee sipping. Instead, there was an electric urgency in the air.

"You find something sturdy enough for a spindle?" Dave asked.

"We located a good solid roof beam, but it's not round," Ben replied. "A spindle has gotta be round, don't it? Not sure if we can make it work or not."

"Don't matter," Dave said. "I've got a chain saw in the truck. I'll round it off real quick."

Cole leaped ahead of him up in the truck bed and handed down a bright orange, Husqvarna chain saw. Charlie and Ben carried the eight-foot long beam over to the tailgate of Dave's truck while Dave gave the saw one mighty pull and she fired right up. All the noise and smoke momentarily diverted Grace's attention from Higgins, who was just as glad she was noticing something besides him.

Without hesitation Dave trimmed the four edges of the beam along the length of it, as Charlie and Ben slowly spun the timber for him. "Good enough," Ben shouted above the roar of the saw. Dave shut it off while Cole and Charlie carried the newly rounded spindle back toward the well.

"Before you put it up on the tripods we should tie the rope," Dave said. "Who's good with knots? I've got two thirty-foot ropes here. If one of you guys can splice them together we'll have plenty of line."

Cole stepped up with the confidence of a salty British sailor and started working the two ends of rope together. Meanwhile, Dave sprinted back to his truck and grabbed a fresh piece of two by four lumber. Quickly he fired up the chain saw again and zipped off about a two-foot long chunk.

Back at the well he handed it to Ben and said, "Nail this turn arm real solid on the end of the spindle. I've got to find something to use as a handle."

Higgins had noticed an old axe handle hiding in the weeds while he was trying to keep his mind off Grace. The biting end of it had rusted away long ago. *If it's still solid, it'd be about right for turning a spindle,* he thought. Dave had headed back toward his truck and everybody else was busy with ropes or nailing, so he fluttered over, grabbed what was left of the axe with his talons, and with an old hawk's grunt managed to get airborne and fly it over to the truck bed.

Dave hefted the strong piece of oak and knew it was perfect for his needs. "Thanks, Orville," he said. "'Preciate it."

Higgins was flattered he'd been mistaken for a much younger hawk, but kept it to himself. He knew Dave Flannery had way more important things on his mind just then.

Dave dug his cordless drill out of the toolbox and tightened a steel bit into it with a quick snap of his wrist. Holding the axe handle on his knee he drilled three deep holes in the flat end. "Carry this over to the spindle for me, Orv," he commanded. "I've got some long screws in the glove box. I'll fetch 'em."

Ever so glad to pitch in, Higgins winged the handle over to Ben who didn't seem particularly surprised at a red-tail's presence on the work site. Even being a small help made Higgins feel better. To a hawk there's nothing worse than just standing around gawking and feeling helpless while others work. He could see Grace was a bit put out he had become an integral part of the construction team, while she was forced to stay in standby mode and be idle.

Grace let out a couple of soft whines, inched a foot or so closer, and ran her long tongue around her mouth to catch the slobber. Higgins very much wanted to apologize to her, but there just wasn't time at the moment.

Dave hurried over with a small box of three-inch brass screws. He handed the drill and three screws to Charlie and said, "This old piece of oak is plenty skookum. Screw it in tight to the end of that two by four."

Higgins had never heard the word skookum before and promised himself to Google it when he got back home. He felt it must be jargon of some sort with a nice, flavorful Native American ring to it. From the context though, he was pretty sure it meant "strong."

Meanwhile Cole and Ben had looped one end of the spliced rope around the center of the spindle and tied it off. Then Cole pounded in a couple of nails half way and bent them down snug over the rope, pinning it tight to make sure it wouldn't slip loose.

As soon as the handle was screwed on Dave said, "All done. We just need to wind the rest of the line around the spindle, load it up on the tripods, and give 'er a go."

Quickly the remaining rope was wrapped around the spindle, and with two men on each end, they hoisted it first to their shoulders like solemn pallbearers at a country church funeral. Then, with a loud grunt and arms extended, they swung the spindle up and centered it over the well, resting it gently upon the tripods on either side.

Seeing those four men straining with the weight of the spindle, and marveling at their artful ingenuity, Higgins couldn't help but remember an old American adage: Necessity is the mother of invention. *How true,* he thought. *It's the South Dakota way.*

Start to finish, construction of the winch had taken but twenty minutes.

Chapter Twenty-eight
Toward the Angels

IN THE RED-TAIL CLANS OF SOUTH DAKOTA, females are usually larger than males. They can weigh as much as a pound more, and when full grown a female's wingspan is often two to four inches wider. No doubt evolution, natural selection, and Darwinian monkey business are behind the plan. Scholars have studied it, but there is no truly satisfactory explanation. For reasons unknown, it's pretty much the opposite in humans.

As soon as the winch was in place Beth Flannery climbed out of the car and approached the men. As is sometimes the case, when men get working together, women, inadvertently, can be made to feel excluded. Male red-tails are often guilty of this as well.

While waiting for the winch to be built, Beth had called Memorial Hospital and talked to Linda Wilson, the head emergency room nurse. Beth explained the situation as best she could without knowing the extent or specifics of Kate's injuries. Nurse Linda had been sympathetic and instructed Beth to wrap Kate warmly, make sure her airway was clear, and transport her to the hospital as soon as possible.

Beth had also chatted briefly with Gramma Flannery, reassuring her the rescue was in progress and everything possible was being done. In true pioneer spirit, Gramma was already busily preparing tuna fish sandwiches and hot chicken soup for the rescue team when their work was complete.

Dave had just reached out over the well and grabbed the dangling end of the yellow rope. "This is strong stuff. If it'll hold a steer, it should hold a man easy."

Ben replied, "The first thing is to get one of us safely down the hole and then put Kate into the harness." He turned to Cole. "There are two harnesses in a black plastic bag next to the first-aid kit way in the back. Quick like, go fetch the smaller one. It should be just about right for Kate."

Cole took off running toward the Explorer just as Beth arrived; she stood near her husband, arms folded across her chest, at the edge of the well.

"Usually on these type rescues," Ben explained, "we're doing an airlift into a helicopter; this is pretty much the same procedure except we don't have easy access to the injured person. From what I can see down at the bottom, it's going to be a tight fit, with not much room to maneuver Kate into the sling." He glanced at Dave. "Also, we don't know how much water there is beneath her. If she's floating in deep water it's gonna be difficult. If it's shallow enough to stand up it'll be lots easier."

Just then a huffing Cole arrived, carrying a leather harness with a shiny reinforced metal clip at the top. He handed it to Ben.

"Kate's legs will need to go through these two leg holes." Ben demonstrated by pushing his arm through the slots. "Once her legs are in, she'll be in the right position to sit on the seat here." He spread his hand across the narrow straps forming the seat. "These two Velcro straps need to be secured tightly, one across her tummy, the other over her chest. Once that's done she can be safely hauled up." Ben's eyes roamed from face to face. "Who wants to go down and strap her in?"

"I do," Cole, Charlie, and Dave said, as one.

Even though Higgins had every confidence Orville could do the job, he felt the men would be difficult to convince, so he kept his beak zipped.

Beth, eyes blazing, said, "I'm the smallest and lightest one here, and it will be lots easier for me to move around down there. I'm not afraid of deep water or tight spaces." Her eyes widened, dared them. Defiant. There was to be no arguing with those eyes.

"Makes sense to me," Dave said, his lips tightening. "I'm fine with it."

"Me too," Cole added, staring down at the ground.

"Okay by me," Charlie said. He lifted his baseball cap, rubbed his bald head with a big hand, and then snugged the cap down again. "Let's do it."

"Okay, Beth it is," Ben said, ending the matter. "It's settled. Cole, tie a non-slip loop in the rope for Beth to put her foot in for the ride down. Once we get Kate up here, we'll wrap her in blankets and put her on the back seat of the Explorer."

He turned to Dave. "You'll ride to the hospital in the back seat with her. Cole, no doubt Kate is hypothermic, so as soon as you get her in the Explorer start her on warm oxygen. The Res-Q-Air case is on the other side of the first-aid kit from where the harness was. Once you get the mask on her and the air flowing, Dave can monitor it. Pile the blankets on her, turn the Ford's heater on full blast, and hightail Kate down to Memorial quick as can be. Charlie and I will hoist Beth out of the well and then we'll follow you down to Philip. Any questions?"

What if Kate is dead? What if the well caves in on Beth and Kate? These were the terrible questions no one dared ask, though all had considered the possibilities.

Charlie looked into the well and broke the strained silence. "What's Beth supposed to do with those two ducks down there?"

"Give me your flashlight," Dave said. Quickly he pointed it down at Kate. "Those aren't ducks, just a couple of hawks. They won't bother Beth any."

Cole had fashioned a stout loop at the end of the rope using a standard, non-slip, bowline knot while Ben instructed the group. Dave held Beth's hips tightly from behind while Charlie played a little more rope out so the looped end of it was at ground level. Then, without needing to be directed by the men, Beth took a big breath and fearlessly leaned out, grabbed the rope with both hands, swung her right foot into the loop and was suddenly suspended in space.

Charlie and Cole manned the winch handle while Ben held out the leather harness. Beth let go of the rope with one hand and quickly put her arm through one of the leg holes in the harness before clutching the rope again.

The color in Beth's face had lightened considerably when she stepped into the loop, but her jaw was set and her eyes resolutely fixed on her husband.

"When you get to the water, shout up to us and we'll give you enough line to test the depth," Ben said. "If it's shallow enough to stand up your job will be a lot easier. Oh, one more thing. When you get the harness on her, clip it to the rope's loop. That clip is engineered to hold three hundred pounds and I'm sure the rope is plenty strong."

Beth didn't speak, merely nodding her head to indicate she understood.

While Charlie and Cole strained on the handle, letting the winch slowly unwind under Beth's weight, Dave and Ben held the rope as close to the center of the well as they could manage to avoid bumping the sides of the well and knocking loose debris down on top of Kate.

In a moment Beth was at the surface of the water and head tilted upward, she yelled, "Hold it!"

Ben held the flashlight beam on the top of Kate's head, so Beth could better see the task ahead.

"I don't think it's very deep," Beth called out. "I'm getting out of the loop now."

She gripped the rope tightly with both hands and released her foot from the loop. The rope went slack as Beth splashed into the water. Standing flat-footed on the bottom, the water was at least two inches below her shoulders. The men listened quietly from above while the light played on the drama unfolding forty or fifty feet below ground.

"Mom's here, Kate," Beth said softly. "You're going to be okay. We'll lift you out in just a minute."

With the harness in one hand, Beth shook the contraption out so the leg holes were in the proper position. Taking a big breath she ducked under the murky water and grabbed Kate's ankle. Quickly she slid it into the proper slot. Beth broke the surface, sputtering; immediately she gulped another big breath and went under again. She grabbed the other ankle and pulled it into the other opening. Fortunately, Kate was unconscious, or the pain from her leg injury would no doubt have been excruciating. The fact she didn't react to the pain was mute testimony to the depth of her unconsciousness.

Standing now, Beth pulled the seat up around her daughter's bottom, and then forcefully snapped the metal clip to the center of the foot loop.

"Pull her up about three feet," Beth shouted. As soon as Kate's bottom was clear of the water, Beth deftly secured the two Velcro straps tightly across Kate's stomach and chest. Her head lolled lifelessly forward toward the water, but she was safely in the harness. "Okay," Beth yelled up at the men. "Hoist away."

With Charlie and Cole manning the crank and Ben holding the light, Dave guided the taut rope so it wound around the center of the creaking spindle, keeping their precious load from scraping against the sides of the well. Slowly Kate's feet cleared the water and she started her upward journey toward the glowing angelic light. She had been in the water for almost fourteen hours.

Beth watched from below and as soon as she saw Dave's and Ben's strong arms reach out and grab Kate, she began to cry the pent up tears stored while her husband had talked to Gramma on the phone at the motel in Rapid City, the tears dammed up during the reckless two and a half hour drive back to the ranch, and the tears relentlessly pushed forward while she had patiently watched the men build the winch were suddenly released and allowed to cascade down her cheeks.

The well was dark now except for a small halo of light at the top. Beth stood, legs shaking.

"Are you okay down there, Beth?" Ben's gentle call a moment later brought her back.

Eyes blurry, she smiled upward. "I think so, Officer Dredge. I'm ready to come up soon as you drop the rope down here."

Chapter Twenty-nine
Kissing a Mummy

While Charlie lowered the line back down the well, Beth turned her attention to Orville and Annabelle clinging to the side of the well just opposite from where Kate had been.

"Oh, Orville," Beth said, "thank you for finding Kate and staying with her until we got here. What a brave and marvelous hawk you are."

When Annabelle had flushed herself down the well on top of Orville, he had been attending to Kate. Once he was certain Kate's head was safely out of the water and resting on her backpack, he had turned to help Annabelle. Realizing she had been severely injured when she struck the wall part way down during her flush maneuver, Orville did his best to comfort and reassure her that their rescue was imminent.

He had then asked Higgins to fly back to the truck and hopefully find a rope to be secured at one end and dropped down to him. Orville was concerned that due to his age, Higgins might not be able to get airborne with the weight of a length of rope in his talons; with desperation so close at hand, what else could be done? It would suffice even if Higgins had to fly with one rope end gripped in his talons and drag the remainder along the ground back to the well. "Create the bridges as you arrive at the obstacles," Orville's father used to say.

Orville believed once a rope was lowered and secured, if he took a firm grip with the talons on his uninjured leg and his beak, he might possibly be able to carry Annabelle piggyback up the rope to the surface where medical aid could then be summoned.

Simultaneously it had dawned on Higgins to call the school for help. Orville's original plan was then shelved when Dr. Spud Richfield, Ms. Chawla Ride, and her class of thirty willing student fliers arrived on scene.

In the meanwhile, to save Annabelle from further suffering and possible drowning, Orville had taken a strong purchase on the well's clay wall with the talons of his good leg near the water's surface. With his damaged leg dangling uselessly, and the lower half of his body immersed in cold water, he had managed to transform his upper self into a reasonably dry shelf. He had then coaxed a reluctant Annabelle out of the water, and she had rested on top of him. Despite the shock caused by her fall she had been able to remain relatively warm and safely out of harm's way, thanks to Orville's ingenuity and strength.

But when it came time to tie the school's rescue rope under Kate's armpits, Orville had asked Annabelle to try and support herself temporarily by digging her one good set of talons into the wall. She had tried valiantly, but weakened by shock, had been unable to do so. She surrendered and fell back into the murky water, desperately paddling one leg just to keep herself barely afloat.

After the students' efforts to pull Kate out of the well failed, Orville had once again been in the process of tending to Kate and Annabelle when Higgins's desperate call of warning had sounded, and Orville was forced to abandon them once more to stave off Grace's ferocious attack above ground.

Once Orville was satisfied the students were aloft and safe he had flushed himself again. He had immediately checked Kate, then quickly re-formed a dry shelf out of his own battered body to save a rapidly fading Annabelle. She was so weakened by then, Orville had to duck under the surface and, like a feathered whale emerging from the depths, come up from beneath to lift her on his back out of the water. Of course, it had been necessary for Orville to support his own waterlogged weight plus Annabelle's, and by this time, he too was becoming utterly exhausted and hypothermic.

When Beth held out her hands to him, he and Annabelle collapsed into Beth's saving arms. She cradled both hawks tenderly as she might a neighbor's precious newborn twins just home from the hospital.

Beth, momentarily distracted, allowed the empty harness to land with a soft splash in the water beside her. She shouted, "Plenty! Hold it!"

She carefully placed the shivering Orville and Annabelle onto the seat. Unable to strap them in properly because of their diminutive size, she said, "Hang on, guys. It's almost over. You'll be safe in a moment."

Orville's eyes remained closed and at first he didn't move, but slowly his talons curled around a web of leather. His beak cracked open and he murmured an almost unintelligible, "Thank you, Kate mother. You save Orville and friend."

Annabelle also instinctively grabbed a strap and sensing the hypothermic trance of death, coupled with exhaustion and injury placed on Orville, she snuggled tight to him, willingly sharing her own dwindling body heat. Somehow she gathered enough strength to open a wing and lay it tenderly over him like a warming blanket of love.

"I'm sending two hawks up," Beth called. "Be gentle and wrap them in a blanket. They need medical attention right away. We'll take them to Doc Walters's clinic in Dupree on our way to the hospital."

A few moments later, Ben gently fluff dried Orville and Annabelle with a soft towel, then wrapped them together like feathered twin mummies in a thick, sand-colored blanket. He then carefully placed the pair on the ground next to the well.

Almost immediately, with Charlie, his long legs stoutly braced, straining by himself on the creaking spindle crank, Beth had ridden the rope, her foot securely planted in the loop, back to the surface. As soon as her feet reached ground level Ben reached out, wrapped his arms around her in a strong bear hug, and pulled his best friend's wife safely back to terra firma. Except for being soaking wet, she seemed none the worse for wear.

"The other Explorer is still parked at the river," Ben said. "If you'll drive us over there in Dave's truck and drop us off, then you can drive yourself back to the ranch for dry clothes. Charlie and I best hustle these little guys to Dupree. The one has lost a lot of blood and may not make it. He's as cold as a sheet of ice on a January water trough. If he survives I expect Doc Walters will need to keep him there at least for a few days. Are you gonna be okay to drive yourself down to Philip?"

"I'll be fine," Beth replied. "Doc put a cast on this hawk's leg about a week and a half ago. Kate and Gramma Flannery have been nursing him back to health. His name is Orville and he's a close family friend. I don't know the other hawk, but it appears he or she could be injured too. Tell Doc the Flannery family will cover the cost of their care."

Beth picked up Orville and Annabelle and started walking with Ben toward the Toyota. "Wouldn't it be easier if you and Charlie take Dave's truck and leave it at the river? I'll drive our car back home, check on Gramma, change my clothes, and get myself on to the hospital. Just leave the keys in the truck for Dave."

Beth handed the mummified hawks to Ben then she reached out and briefly caressed Orville's head. "Thank you, Orville," she said. "I'll never forget what you've done for our Kate." In time-worn tradition, Beth paid Orville the highest form of human gratitude and affection she possibly could. Leaning down, she gently kissed the side of his beak.

Despite the chill of death placed on him by the night's ordeal, Orville's eyes flickered open for an instant; his beak shivered, tried valiantly to open, but nary a peep came out.

Ben turned to Charlie and said, "Toss Grace up in the back of Ben's truck and we'll head on out. In a day or two we'll get a crew out here to put a cement cap on this rat-trap of a well. I'd sure like to know who took the cover off it in the first place. Dang near as bad as putting a gun on someone and pulling the trigger."

A moment later Charlie lifted Grace up into the bed of the pick-up and climbed in front with Ben. He gently placed Orville and Annabelle, still wrapped like mummies, on the seat between them.

"Grace got herself bloodied up somehow." He glanced over at his partner. "Got dried blood all over my hands from her belly when I picked her up just now."

"Wonder how that happened," Ben replied, releasing the parking brake.

"Don't rightly know," Charlie said. "Maybe one of those hawks got to her somehow. They really skedaddled when Grace came rushing down off the butte toward the well. I figure Grace smelled Kate's baseball cap from clear up there. Pretty amazing what she can do with her nose. We'd have spent at least another hour or so searching before we'd found the well without Grace. By then it mighta been too late to save Kate. I'm hoping they get her down to Memorial before it's—well—you know."

As much as Higgins was apprehensive about riding in the back alone with Grace, he was left little choice. It was either share the ride or just wing it on home, not knowing the fate of Orville and Annabelle. As their former flight instructor and now friend forevermore, going on home without them was not an option.

When the truck started to turn toward the river, Higgins launched himself and took a comfortable seat in the back as far away from Grace as possible. She appeared healthy enough, but you never knew what kind of germs a dog might pick up, nosing around on the ground like they do. Years ago when Higgins was a fledgling, his mother would warn him about getting too close to those critters. According to her, socializing with a dog was even riskier than playing with sharp sticks or flying with a pair of scissors.

Old baggage aside, the opportunity to ride in the back of a Ford pickup and visit a vet's office for the first time outweighed his natural hesitation to hobnob with Grace. Higgins tried to ignore the deep growl in her throat, and explain to her as best he could what had happened before she arrived at the rescue scene.

Grace's mood softened and the growls ceased upon hearing Higgins's explanation. Soon enough she curled up, nose to tail, and fell fast asleep. Dogs can jump nap, no matter the place, time, or weather. It's an enviable talent they have. *Somebody should bottle it,* thought Higgins.

Chapter Thirty

Sticks and Stones May Break My Bones

THE IRON MOUNTAIN RED-TAIL COMMUNITY HAD heard rumors of the so-called bird flu epidemic, mostly in southeast Asia, and more recently, the swine flu scare. As with all germs, they find their way to South Dakota soon enough. In Minnesota, the neighbor to the east, a few crows had mysteriously died in the past couple of months. It took a lot to kill a crow, so this flu bug was nothing to mess with. Most hawks were keeping their shots up to date, just in case. One should never be too careful with crows, viruses, or dogs.

Dr. Packard appeared too young to be a doctor. In fact he was thirty-nine, but good genes and a healthy life style distorted his true age into a fuzzy, almost meaningless number. Curious blue eyes and an ever-present grin signaled his zest for living. A buzz haircut, perfectly straight teeth, the obligatory doctor's white coat, shiny brown cowboy boots, and a black stethoscope draped casually around his neck like a thin rubber boa completed the picture.

On this particular Saturday, the emergency room waiting area was unusually quiet. Normally the room would be packed with violently ill or severely injured patients anxiously waiting their turn to be seen. The Rapid Response Vehicle, parked in the scanty shade created by the two-story brick building, lingered just outside the main door, at the ready for the next emergency call.

Dave and Beth stood up from the comfortable sofa as the doctor approached. "Mom and Dad Flannery, I presume?" As his boyish grin widened into a welcoming smile, he extended his hand first to Beth, then to Dave. "Glad to meet you," he said, "I'm Mack Packard and I've got good news. First though, I want to give a big bravo to you both for helping pull Kate out of that well. Just getting her out must have been a huge job. My hat is off to you and the sheriff's team."

Dr. Packard gently took Beth's elbow and guided her back toward the sofa where the three of them sat side by side.

"Okay, here it is. Kate must have been immersed in fairly cold water for several hours. On arrival she was extremely hypothermic. We're still in the process of warming her up and giving her fluids. The sheriff's deputy has access to a Res-Q-Air machine so Kate was given heated and humidified oxygen during the transport from the accident site to here, and this made all the difference. We started a warm IV drip immediately to help raise her core temperature. We don't know how much well water she swallowed so just to be safe we've added an antibiotic. Germs like wet, dark places."

Dr. Packard's calm demeanor lent the impression he dealt with people trapped in wells almost on a daily basis.

"She also just got back from X-ray and she has a closed fracture of her right tibia. When she fell into the well she must have landed awkwardly on her leg somehow. It's a fairly severe break and we're going to have to go in and check it in surgery later this afternoon.

"The best news is even though hypothermia and a broken leg are serious medical problems, they're both treatable and we expect one hundred percent recovery. Kate is a young and healthy kid so she'll bounce back from these two issues very quickly. She is conscious, but still quite groggy. She hasn't said much but has mumbled something about someone named Orville a couple of times. I'd say she's coming along as well as can be expected after what she's been through. I'm sure she's going to be just fine in a few days. Any questions?"

Dave said, "You mentioned a closed fracture of her leg. What exactly is that?"

"Kate broke her tibia, more commonly known as the shin bone in the lower leg. A closed fracture simply means the skin adjacent to the fractured bone was not broken. Sometimes with severe fractures, like the one your daughter suffered, the sharp end of the broken bone will poke out through the skin, and potentially create all kinds of serious infection problems. Fortunately it didn't happen in this case. Kate's type of injury is not as likely to become infected or have serious tissue damage because the bone ends did not make contact with the well water or outside air. It's still a very serious break, but one we and our good friend time can remedy."

"How long will she be in a cast?" Beth asked. "School starts soon and I know she won't want to miss a single day."

Dr. Packard laughed. "I wish my two boys were so enthusiastic about school. Normally we think six to eight weeks in a cast. I imagine she's going to be on crutches until just before Halloween. If she has an upstairs bedroom you may want to relocate her downstairs for a while to save her going up and down stairs with the crutches. Easy to get tangled up and take another spill hopping on one leg up and down stairs."

"You mentioned surgery?" Beth asked. "How serious is that?"

"Well, any surgery is serious and I don't want to minimize the risk, but it's a pretty straightforward procedure. We'll give her a spinal anesthesia and make a three or four inch incision through the skin and tissue right above the break. I've already manipulated the two bone ends back into place, but I need to make certain they're lined up perfectly and adjust them if need be. While I'm in there I'll also see if any serious tissue damage occurred during the rescue or transport, but I don't expect I'll find much. In the worst-case scenario I may have to put in a pin or a small plate, but I doubt that.

"The X-rays didn't reveal any significant impact damage requiring a pin. Actually, the cold water in the well likely was quite beneficial in helping keep the swelling down and tissue damage to a minimum. She'll have a tiny scar on her leg the rest of her life. Anything else?"

Dave spoke up. "We really appreciate your care of Kate, Dr. Packard. Thanks a lot for taking the time to explain all this to us." Dave stood up and extended his hand.

Dr. Packard glanced at his watch. "I've scheduled her surgery for two o'clock this afternoon. The procedure will take an hour at most so after she's out of the OR and back in her room you can drop in and stay with her as long as you like. If everything goes as it should, I think young Kate will most likely be able to go home late Monday morning."

"Thank you so much, Dr. Packard," Beth said.

The young physician had taken no more than three quick steps away when he whirled around. Running a hand through his short hair he said, "I forgot something. During our initial examination we found rope burns under Kate's armpits. I immediately asked the county deputy who drove her in here about the rescue operation, and he said a standard lift harness was used and the rope never actually touched her. Any idea how she might have gotten rope burns?"

Dave said, "Burns in her armpits don't make any sense at all. Like Cole told you, we used one of their rescue harnesses and the rope was clipped to it above her head."

Beth added, "I fastened the rope to a metal clip on the harness. I don't know what could have caused rope burns."

"Well," Dr. Packard said, "it's not really important, but I'm curious about how it happened. Maybe Kate will be able to tell us about it when she's fully conscious."

Chapter Thirty-one
Silly Words of Love

Late Monday afternoon, the Flannerys pulled into the vet clinic's shade free parking lot in the Toyota. Kate was sitting sideways on the back seat, her right leg propped up on two hospital pillows Nurse Linda insisted they borrow for the ride back home. Kate, already into the third chapter of *To Kill a Mockingbird,* gently closed the book. "I guess I'll wait here," she said.

"It's going to get awfully hot in the car," Dave said. "Why don't you test drive your new crutches and come in with us? I'm sure Doc Walters would like to see you again."

Kate carefully slid her left leg out the car door down to the gravel lot. Her parents watched anxiously as she held on to the door edge and gingerly stood up, balancing precariously on her good leg. Dave handed her the crutches and Kate tentatively slipped them under her armpits. She flashed a smile and said, "How do I look?"

"Wonderful," Beth said.

"Like an Afghanistan war vet home on leave," said Dave. "C'mon, girls, it's hot out here."

In a moment the three of them were standing in Doc Walters's waiting room. His wife and receptionist, Mary Walters, peered up at them from over the tops of her glasses. "Hi, Flannerys," she said. "Did you come to fetch your hawk colony?"

Dave grinned. "Hi, Mary. What do you mean, colony? How many are there?"

"Well, there are two young ones, Orville and Annabelle, and there was another old timer who called himself Higgins something or other, but I guess he got tired of snooping around and finally flew off home."

"Wow!" Kate said, her eyes lighting up. "They must be Orvie's family or something. Is Orville okay? Mom said he was completely out of it when he was lifted out of the well."

Before Mary could reply, Doc Walters emerged from the back room drying his hands on a paper towel. "Thought I heard you Flannerys out here." He grinned. "Well, I hear someone fell into a well and broke her leg. Any truth to that rumor, Kate Flannery?"

He gave her braid the customary church bell tug. "A well is a rather strange place to read, isn't it? Most of the ones I've been in don't have much light and are a bit damp. Tends to make the pages kinda limp, don't it?"

Mary let out a derisive snort from her little office and said, "Kate Flannery, don't you believe a word he says. I never seen a man who likes to tell stories half as much as he does. Fibs is more like it."

Not bothering to deny the charges, Doc Walters rubbed his hands together and laughed out loud. He wheeled around and greeted Beth and Dave with an extended hand. "Hi, Beth. Hi, Dave. Glad everything turned out okay. Tell you what—those doctors up at Philip are first rate, ain't they? No need to drive clear over to Rapid City, when such good care is nearby. Mary and I do all our doctoring up there at Memorial."

Then rotating back to Kate, he said, "Can I be the first to autograph your cast?"

Kate, suddenly shy, blushed and said, "Sure, I guess so."

Doc Walters dropped to his knees, pulled a ball point pen out of his shirt pocket, leaned over and writing sideways, scribbled: *To the best reader, fishergirl, and wellfaller in all of South Dakota from the oldest and onlyest vet in Dupree. Mooingly Yours, Miles Walters, DVM.*

"Nothing better than being the first one on the plaster. Except my darling wife's pie crust, I mean." He smiled mischievously at Mary, who was pretending to attend to more important matters than listening to her silly husband fabricate more fibs.

Holding onto the reception counter with one hand, and with a slight grunt, he slowly pulled himself back to his feet. "I suppose you'd like to pick up Orville and his friend? C'mon in the back. They don't say much and they're well behaved, I'll give them that. Pretty much ideal patients. No complaining at all. Not like cats. Cats'll even gripe about the music on the radio. Don't make sense to me, but some of 'em don't like country. Can you imagine?"

The small group paraded along behind the old doctor back to his work area. On a long stainless steel counter running the length of one wall in the small room, rested two identical shallow wicker baskets about half the size of a typical laundry basket. In the bottom of each lay a fluffy white bath towel folded in thirds.

In the first one, Annabelle lay on her side gazing over at Orville. Her right leg, from hip to just above her talons, sported a shiny white cast and was resting on a small homemade pink satin pillow. In the second Orville lay on his side facing Annabelle. His right leg also featured a fresh white cast, but near the hip and talons two short metal pins about an inch long protruded through the plaster. A third, longer rod connected the two pins on the outside of the cast. The whole apparatus was carefully balanced on a small blue pillow.

"Hi, guys," Doc Walters said. "You've got visitors."

Both hawks swiveled their heads to take in the assembled Flannery family. "Hi, Orvie," Kate said. She reached out and softly stroked his head. "Guess what? I broke my leg too. I have to walk with crutches for a month or so. Who's your friend?"

Orville, suddenly bashful, didn't answer, so Doc Walters said, "I think her name is Annabelle. Can't quite catch her last name. Might be Mathis or Matthews. She's a real shy one." He reached out and touched Annabelle's cast. "Wonder what the odds are of having two red-tailed hawks and a girl with a golden braid suffering broken legs all at the same time?"

"She was the other hawk down in the well with you and Orville, honey," Beth said. "I don't have any idea how or why she ended up in the well, but she rode the harness up to the surface just like you did—except she had her eyes wide open. She even wrapped her wing around Orville to make sure he didn't fall."

Beth glanced quickly at her husband. "Reminds me," she said, "when they brought you into the hospital Dr. Packard discovered some rope burns under your armpits. That confused the doctor and us because I hooked the rope to a clip on the harness above your head—the rope never actually touched you. Do you remember anything about a rope being wrapped around you?"

Kate slowly shook her head. "I remember waking up in the well. It was really dark and freaky, but after a while when I realized the water wasn't too deep and I stopped being afraid of drowning, I sort of zoned out. I don't remember anything about a rope. I didn't see one."

Just then Orville, unable to contain himself any longer, partially opened one wing. He tried hard to sit up, but his leg was immobilized and he couldn't get the necessary leverage. He slowly lifted his head from the towel and looked right into Doc's eyes for a long moment. Then, trembling with the effort, he allowed his head to sink back to the towel.

Doc said thoughtfully, "It appears the hawks organized a rescue attempt to pull Kate from the well. Anyway, that's what I think he said."

Dave added, "Sounds right. Charlie told me when he and Grace first arrived at the well he saw a flock of hawks take off, maybe twenty or thirty of 'em. I thought it kinda strange because I've never heard of hawks traveling in a flock before. Whenever I see 'em they're usually flying alone. Once in a while I might see two together. Charlie said he thought they were carrying a long rope or maybe some string with them. Hard to believe, but what else could it be?"

Kate said, "I believe it. I'll bet Orvie somehow called all his school buddies and they used a rope to try and pull me out." She continued to tenderly stroke Orville's head.

Dr. Walters smiled thoughtfully. "I've been doctoring animals for over fifty years, and never a day goes by one of 'em doesn't amaze me somehow. Wish I could have seen all them hawks straining, wings beating like crazy. Would have been something to remember forever. People just don't realize how smart these critters are. We can learn a lot from 'em if we'd pay a little more attention."

He reached up and scratched the back of his head. "When Ben and Charlie brought Orville and Annabelle in here Saturday morning there was a third hawk along. Nothing medically wrong with him, no broken legs even, but he was a curious old bird for sure. At the time, Orville's body temperature and blood pressure had dropped to the point where he needed critical care immediately or we were gonna lose him, so I was real busy there for an hour or so. Anyway, this other hawk sat around all morning back here perched on the counter watching Mary and me work on Orville and Annabelle. Almost like he was their guardian angel or something. All I could get out of him was his name—Higgins—or something pretty close to that. RT Boyd Higgins sounds like. Seemed smart as a country church preacher, and tried to help anyway he could. It wasn't so much he was too shy, it was more like he was just reticent to interrupt our work. After I got Orville's blood pressure stabilized and we were putting those pins in Orville's leg, Mary and I were busy so Higgins even moved the spotlight for us when we needed a fifth hand." Doc shook his head like he could hardly believe it himself.

"After we finished with the surgery we packed blankets and hot water bottles around both of them; Higgins kept checking all day long to make sure the water was warm and Orville and Annabelle were covered properly."

"What happened to him?" Dave asked. "I'll bet it was the same hawk who helped me build the handle for the winch out at the well. At the time I thought it was Orville, but it couldn't have been because he was down in the well with Kate. I'll bet Higgins was the one who gathered all the hawks to try and pull Kate out of the well."

"More than likely," Doc Walters replied. "Well, once we got these two patched up, he followed me outside to the pens and I told him about a couple of hard cases I'm treating out there. Are you familiar with Les Riley's bull, Churchill? Meanest bull in Ziebach County, bar none. He's been sick for about a week now, and every time I get near him he tries to flat out murder me. Also, Widow Parks's old milk cow, Winifred, has been trying her best to die for a long time. I believe Winnie's close to three hundred years old."

Doc chuckled. "And Widow Parks isn't a whole lot younger. Well, Higgins didn't say much, but he seemed mighty interested in all the particulars. Asked me why I didn't let nature take its course with those two cows.

'Just let 'em go, Doc,' he said. 'For sure they'd be lots happier.' He meant it too.

"After we came back in here he studied all my equipment—even went out in the waiting room and poked about. Never seen a hawk interested in *National Geographic* pictures before, turning the pages with his beak like it was something he does every day. I seen people sit out there for two hours and never once open up one of those magazines. Lots of 'em would rather just twiddle their thumbs and whine about how slow old Doc Walters is rather than try to learn a little something. No wonder the Chinese are about to take over the world."

Doc shook his head, his eyes glistening. "Mary gave Higgins a stale Oreo cookie she's been saving out there for about ten years. He came back in here, hopped up on the counter, and mused over our two sleeping beauties. After about ten minutes just sitting and watching 'em sleep, he leaned down—strangest thing I ever saw—he touched the side of his beak to Annabelle's beak and then to Orville's. I guess he was sort of kissing them good-bye or something. A few minutes later Mary and I were fixing to close up and walk home for dinner, and he just up and followed us out the door. He came along as far as the edge of the parking lot; then he came over to me and rubbed the side of his beak on my shoe. I'll tell you, it prickled my neck with a real bad case of industrial strength goose bumps."

Doc slowly rubbed the back of his neck with his hand like he wanted to feel those goose bumps and cherish them once more.

"In this business, Dave, I shake hands with a lot of people when I'm done with my work. Mary and me, well we ain't never been rich, but we got all we ever need, you know what I mean? Put three kids through school and all. Comfortable, is what I call it. Higgins rubbing his beak on my shoe gave me a wonderful feeling—almost like he was saying, 'Thank you very much, Doc Walters. I truly appreciate what you've done for us today.' His eyes blinked real fast, just like I do from time to time when I get a lumpy throat feeling, and just like that, he was gone. He sailed off and vanished into the sky before I could say a word. Gorgeous red tail feathers on those birds."

He rested a hand on Annabelle, gently stroking her head. "Well, I was standing there all teary eyes, fighting a big ol' throat lump, and good wife Mary pulling my arm out of its socket, yanking me along toward our dinner; all I could do was watch him disappear, and wonder who he was and how he was related to these two hawks here. Wondering all the time if I'd ever see him again."

"Do you think Higgins is Orville's or Annabelle's dad or maybe uncle?" Kate asked. Her voice was almost a whisper, and her eyes glowed, catching a flaming remnant of dying light streaming in the windows.

"Could be, I suppose," Doc Walters replied. "But somehow I think he's just fond of them like a good friend would be and wanted to make certain they were all right. He's connected to them somehow, but then, so are we. We're all alive in this together, young Kate, don't you see?" He turned his head and stared out the window for a moment before saying, "I know I'll never forget Higgins, or either of these two red-tails."

"Well," Dave said, "it's getting late and I'm sure you and Mary would like to get on home. It's been a long couple of days and we need to get back to the ranch to make sure Gramma Flannery is okay. She had herself quite an adventure with Orville, what I hear. I'm kinda curious about how my truck ended up in the river." He picked up the basket containing Orville.

Orville's beak opened wide and a funny sounding hawk giggle flowed out, something like ice cubes dropping into an empty glass, at the memory of Gramma driving down the bank and into the river. *Lord what fools these mortals be,* he thought, puckish as ever.

Dave laughed at Orville's obvious delight. He reached for his back pocket, but before he could dig his wallet out, Doc Walters grabbed his arm and said, "The costs for the plaster, the anesthesia, and the two paper clips I cut up for the brace on Orville's leg were almost nothing, Dave. Don't worry, I'll bruise you plenty next time one of your calves is born rump first. You Flannerys get on home now. This one's on me."

Dave and Beth thanked him, and Beth said, "Thanks for everything, Dr. Walters. We can't thank you enough for all you've done for our family, and for all the people and animals in this county. Birds too. Soon as Kate gets back to school and I get myself organized, I'm going to sketch a well scene with those young hawks straining to pull Kate out. You'll be getting a framed pen and ink come Christmas time."

Kate leaned her new crutches against the counter—hopping, pirate-like, on her one good leg—to share a shy hug with Doc Walters.

"You're the coolest vet ever," Kate said. "Thanks for taking such good care of Orvie and Annabelle for me.

I'm going to be just like you someday. I promise."

Doc Walters stuck out his hand. "Shake on it?"

Later, up on the highway headed west toward Red Elm, Beth squinched herself over tight as she could to her husband's side, a wicker basket resting on the seat beside her. Inside the basket, Annabelle lay on her side, head turned to see the more; she stared longingly up at a half-eaten ice cream cone in Beth's hand.

In the back seat Kate had her leg propped up on a fluffy pile of borrowed hospital pillows; on her lap was balanced a second wicker basket. Orville grinned up at Kate and she smiled back at him.

To Kill a Mockingbird waited patiently within easy reach. To say Orville had more than a passing interest in the title of such a book would be an understatement. He intended to find out the details as soon as possible.

Already way too much killing in this world, he thought.

Chapter Thirty-two
Loose Ends

AFTER ORVILLE AND ANNABELLE SPENT NEARLY two months recuperating at the Flannery ranch with Kate and the rest of the Flannery family caring for them, their initial fondness for each other bloomed into a raging wildfire romance. They've since married and Annabelle has hatched four beautiful nestlings: Shaw, Delta, Owen, and Fofanna. Three of the four must wear sunglasses during the daytime, but the youngest, Fofanna, apparently has laser sharp vision just like her mother's. For the record, red-tails mate for life.

For now, Annabelle is home schooling her brood, but Orville has already registered the oldest two, Shaw and Delta, at the Prairie Winds School of Flight. He can't wait for RT Chawla Ride to sharpen her talons on his fledglings and help them become special flyers.

Orville, like most sensible males, finally yielded to wifely pressure, and now sports a classic pair of gunmetal grey Maui Jim Kapalua 502 sunglasses secured to his head by a red Velcro strap for his daily hunting expeditions. It's a terrific look on him. According to a reputable source, the Ziebach County sheriff's office, out of gratitude for Orville's unselfish acts related to Kate's rescue, took up a collection and paid the sizeable tab for the sunglasses.

The National Teachers Association awarded Scholastic Gold Medals of Honor to Ms. Chawla Ride and Dr. Spud Ridgefield for leading the Prairie Winds School of Flight's senior class in their daring rescue attempt of Kate.

Also, the South Dakota state board of education awarded silver medals of commendation to each of the students under Ms. Ride's direction. The students were also treated to a trip out to California and Disneyland during their spring break. For most of them it was their first time out of South Dakota, and also their first airplane ride.

Doc Walters has slowed down some, cutting back on his office hours, but is generally well and continues his veterinary practice in Dupree. His wife Mary passed on last spring of a heart attack.

Now and then, Doc and Higgins meet for breakfast—coffee and a short stack of blueberry hotcakes at The Ranch House, a nice little café in Dupree. Real friendly service and right good food. Folks there are getting used to seeing Higgins perched on a child's booster seat across from Doc, and don't think much of it anymore. Like the sign says when you drive off the main road into town, *Dupree is a nice place to hang your hat.*

With Mary gone and more time on his hands, Doc's become attached to a game of logic called Sudoku printed every day in the morning paper. He and Higgins sometimes sit, sip coffee, and put their heads together to solve the more difficult puzzles. Doc is way better at it than Higgins.

Grace, the black lab, and Higgins remain civil, but not close. You know him and dogs. Labs, despite their famously sunny dispositions, have been known to carry grudges, and Higgins sincerely regrets he and Grace had a confrontation. Like Doc Walters says though, "Stuff happens."

Gramma Flannery still dabbles in poetry and remains a loyal Chicago Cubs fan to the bitter end. This year's team, despite spending a lot of money for a hotshot manager and a couple of sluggers, offers scant hope—the usual pitching problems. Still, Cubs fans, like South Dakotans in general, never give up.

A long overdue collection of Gramma's poetry, titled *Words To Fill the Silo,* will hit the stores next spring. Almost all of Gramma Flannery's poems rhyme and have a pleasant heartbeat. It's doubtful *The New Yorker* critics will like them though. Takes all kinds.

Beth and Dave Flannery continue to be the epitome of modern South Dakota homesteaders—kind, hardworking, and generous to a fault. The ranch thrives, not so much because of the land's genial willingness, but rather, because of the Flannery's stubborn insistence it do so.

About a week after Kate's rescue, the county sent out a work crew with a couple of dump truck loads full of dirt and rubble to fill in the abandoned well. They also poured a concrete cap on top to seal it off once and for all. Dave Flannery soon affixed a shiny brass sign to the concrete.

Composed by Gramma Flannery, it reads:

> *To all who traipse by*
> *Björn Dahl's dismal well,*
> *And wonder how or why*
> *Kate Flannery fell—*
> *And how a brave hawk,*
> *One Orville by name,*
> *Gamely walked the walk,*
> *'Til the county came:*
> *'Tis a marvelous good secret, well kept,*
> *While all around, unknowing, the world slept.*

> Susan Flannery
> September 8, 2012

On the first Christmas morning after the adventure, Dave, Beth, Gramma, and Kate showed up out at Higgins's place with a beautiful, framed copy of the pen and ink drawing Beth had promised Doc Walters. Beth drew the scene almost exactly as Higgins witnessed it; it shows thirty-two hawks welded to a thin rope, their wings desperately thrashing the air above a dark hole in the ground, with Higgins standing, peering down into the well.

Higgins home is quite small, and as much as he cherishes Beth's drawing, he donated it to the Prairie Winds School of Flight, where it hangs in the school foyer to greet all visitors. Doc Walters has the original mounted above the fireplace in his home.

Finally, Kate Flannery's leg healed well enough for her to play on the Dupree Middle School volleyball team, and she plans to run cross-country next fall. She reads more than ever and still maintains a four point in school. Her mates have recently elected her senior class president, so her fears of becoming a social outcast apparently are over. Those dreadful episodes of name-calling and bullying are done with. Kate turns seventeen in two weeks and is tall and slim like her parents. She wears her hair short now and heads turn wherever she goes. Deputy Charlie's son, Chris, has big eyes on Kate. Of course attraction goes both ways. Almost always does.

Orville, Annabelle, and their four youngsters regularly visit Kate at the Flannery ranch. Friends forevermore, indeed!

Last time Kate texted Doc Walters, she said her sights are firmly set on veterinary medicine and someday taking over a small clinic in Dupree, not far from the Flannery ranch. You know the one. To get a jumpstart, she works Saturdays for Doc Walters as his office receptionist and assistant. No doubt about it, she'll make a crackerjack vet.

Acknowledgements

THE WORDS AND IDEAS IN THIS STORY ARE MINE alone, but it never would have seen daylight had it not been for my editors at WiDo Publishing to whom I owe so much—to Allie Maldonado who saw a glimmer of possibility where others saw none; to Summer Ross who cheerfully kicked aside the stones to better see the nuggets; and to master seamstress Karen Gowen who snipped the fabric and stitched the ragged edges together.

For their inspiration, a lifetime of laughter and insight from steadfast friends, Ray, Doug, Phil, Dale, Roland, Mik, Barb, Terri and Chie-san.

For their love, a writer's fire, my sisters, Patti, Judy and Sandy.

For her memory and giggles, Pam.

Finally, the unwavering encouragement, support, and love of my darling wife, Norizan, allowed me to forge ahead when I might have given up.

I share the honor with these.

—John E. Irby

About the Author

John E. Irby grew up and was educated in Seattle. After a four-year stint in the navy as a hospital corpsman, he took his bachelor's degree in American and British literature at the University of Washington. For the next thirty years he taught Language Arts to seventh and ninth graders. In retirement, when not writing or reading, he enjoys long walks and international travel with his wife Norizan. *Red-Tailed Rescue* is his first novel.

CPSIA information can be obtained at www.ICGtesting.com
Printed in the USA
BVOW08s1137090214

344397BV00003B/47/P